PUFFIN BOOKS

TUCHUS & TOPPS INVESTIGATE THE ATTACK OF THE ROBOT LIBRARIANS

Other titles by
SAM COPELAND &
JENNY PEARSON

THE UNDERPANTS OF CHAOS

Other titles by
SAM COPELAND

CHARLIE CHANGES INTO A CHICKEN

CHARLIE TURNS INTO A T-REX

CHARLIE MORPHS INTO A MAMMOTH

UMA AND THE ANSWER
TO ABSOLUTELY EVERYTHING

GRETA AND THE GHOST HUNTERS

Other titles by
JENNY PEARSON

THE SUPER MIRACULOUS JOURNEY
OF FREDDIE YATES

THE INCREDIBLE RECORD SMASHERS

GRANDPA FRANK'S GREAT BIG BUCKET LIST

OPERATION NATIVITY

TUCHUS & TOPPS INVESTIGATE

THE ATTACK OF THE ROBOT LIBRARIANS

SAM COPELAND   JENNY PEARSON

Illustrated by ROBIN BOYDEN and KATIE KEAR

PUFFIN

PUFFIN BOOKS

UK | USA | Canada | Ireland | Australia
India | New Zealand | South Africa

Puffin Books is part of the Penguin Random House group of companies
whose addresses can be found at global.penguinrandomhouse.com.

www.penguin.co.uk
www.puffin.co.uk
www.ladybird.co.uk

Penguin
Random House
UK

First published 2023

001

Printed and bound in Great Britain by Clays Ltd, Elcograf S.p.A.

A CIP catalogue record for this book is available from the British Library

The authorized representative in the EEA is Penguin Random House Ireland,
Morrison Chambers, 32 Nassau Street, Dublin D02 YH68

ISBN: 978-0-241-52705-4

All correspondence to:
Puffin Books, Penguin Random House Children's
One Embassy Gardens, 8 Viaduct Gardens, London SW11 7BW

MIX
Paper from
responsible sources
FSC® C018179

Penguin Random House is committed to a
sustainable future for our business, our readers
and our planet. This book is made from Forest
Stewardship Council® certified paper.

To the huge artistic talents
that are Robin Boyden,
Katie Kear and Ben Hughes,
who help bring our books to life.

PROLOGUE

AGATHA

My name is Agatha Topps and I am a spy-detective. Before last year, I preferred to work alone, but then Lenny Tuchus showed up and I took him on as an assistant. I'll admit I had my doubts, but when strange things started happening at our school, Little Strangehaven Primary, I was glad to have him by my side. Most of the time.

I mean, it wasn't ideal when he almost had us floating off into space. And, while it wasn't *completely* his fault, I think he was a little to blame for us almost getting strangled by our own underpants. He does also struggle with a lot of the basic skills required to be an excellent spy-detective. Like slinking down corridors and generally being quiet. And let's just say that some of his ideas are a little questionable. For instance, for a long time, he thought the source of the Strangeness was his belly-button mole, Bernard.

But, while he wouldn't necessarily have been my first choice of assistant, he *did* stop me from being sucked into the *Book of Chaos* and save our town from total destruction. The book, you see, turned out to be the source of all the Strangeness. Luckily, we got rid of it *and* Mr Pardon – our old school librarian who was using it for evil.

We did gain Gregor, though. Gregor is a Scottish gargoyle that the *Book of Chaos* brought to life and Lenny and I sort of adopted. I wouldn't say he's *exactly* like a pet, but he is a big responsibility. He requires constant feeding and occasional grooming to stop the Creeping Crevice Moss in his butt crack from becoming a bum sore.

With the book gone, we thought that Little Strangehaven would go back to normal, but, as is always the way, when one enemy is vanquished, another raises its head. Or, in this case, heads. The beginning of Year Five saw Lenny and me facing a whole new threat. A company called Minerva, owned by one Pamela Stranglebum, had been brought into Little Strangehaven Primary to modernize the library with their tiny robot-owl librarians.

Tiny robot-owl librarians – sound kind of cute, right?

WRONG!

At first, the worst thing the owls did was select terrible and boring books that were meant to make us cleverer. But they soon moved on. Before long, they were monitoring our behaviour with their laser-red eyes. Then they started doling out punishments for minor rule-breaking, like running in the corridor or being late for lessons. That was bad enough, but I just had this *feeling* that there was something even more sinister behind them.

It turned out my spy-detective senses were right on point and soon Lenny and I were deep into our second mission – to stop the attack of the robot librarians!

CHAPTER 1

LENNY

'I hate sequels,' whispered Agatha. 'They're never as good as the original.'

Our class was shuffling into assembly, and we were whispering about the new superhero movie, *Revengers II: The Really Long War*. As it was the start of the school year, everybody had brand-new stuff – lunch boxes, pencil cases and baggy uniforms. My new trousers were *sooooo* long. Mum said it was to give me room to grow, but I'd tripped over them three times on the way to school. I looked even more ridiculous standing next to

Agatha, who was going for the ankle-grazing look. She caught me looking from my trousers to hers.

'My parents didn't have time to get me new ones,' she blurted out.

I shrugged, then turned to Ernie Strewdel and whispered, 'Have you seen *Revengers* yet, Ern?'

Ernie nodded enthusiastically as we sat down. 'Yes! It was great. I was totally surprised by who the bad guy turned out to be!'

'Don't tell me!' I said. 'My dad was supposed to take me, but he got very busy with work.'

Agatha raised an eyebrow. 'For the whole of the summer holidays?'

I was about to tell her that she should know that the life of an MI5 agent is a busy one, but she shushed me and nodded up at the ceiling. Perched on the rafters were two of the Minerva robot-owl librarians, which the headmaster, Dr Errno, had introduced last year. Their eyes were glowing red and they were scanning everybody for bad behaviour.

A look of terror crossed Ernie's face, which is only to be expected because not everybody can be a super-brave spy-detective like me.

Agatha tapped me on the shoulder and I let out a courageous scream of warning. The robot owls swung their heads, their eyes focusing on me. I gulped but, luckily for me, a couple of new Year Three kids were still chatting happily away to each other. One of the owls' warning alarms sounded. **'UNAUTHORIZED TALKING! UNAUTHORIZED TALKING!'**

Then the owls swooped down and dive-bombed the new kids. All they could do was wail as owly beaks clamped on to their collars. The rest of the school watched as they were pulled to their feet and hauled out of the assembly hall. Absolute silence fell.

'Let that be a warning to you all,' Dr Errno said, leaning forward on his lectern. 'At Little Strangehaven, we expect exemplary behaviour at all times or you will be undertaking a repentance task.'

Repentance tasks are THE WORST! Trust me, I've done loads of them. I once had to clean the school chickens' feet with a tiny toothbrush because I left one muddy footprint in a corridor. Another time, I spent ages handwashing all the stinky lost PE kit because I'd forgotten my gym shorts. The robot owls hover above you while you do the tasks and if you stop, even for a second, they'll land on top of your head and peck you until you start again.

As I fumed at the thought of the horrible robot

owls, Agatha pointed to the stage. 'That looks like trouble,' she whispered darkly.

Standing behind Dr Errno was a man I'd never seen before. He was wearing tiny shorts and a T-shirt and had really long legs.

My spy-detective antennae started going crazy. There was something wrong about this guy. You should never trust somebody who wears tiny shorts after summer; they're always angry because they have cold legs.

'Who's he?' I whispered.

'Who's who?' Agatha whispered back.

'The man in the tiny shorts.'

'Never mind the man in the *really* far-too-tiny shorts. Look who's *next* to him!'

I moved my eyeballs slightly to the left, and saw who Agatha was pointing at. It was none other than Pamela Stranglebum, whose company, Minerva, was responsible for the robot-owl librarians now making everyone's life a misery. I fumed some more.

'*What's she doing back here?*' Agatha asked.

What's she doing back here? I thought, just after Agatha said it, which was annoying because I'd wanted to say it first.

Dr Errno flared his impossibly large nostrils and the silence in the hall got even silenter.

'Now, children,' Dr Errno said, 'I'd like you to welcome two people today. The first –' he pointed to the man in the tiny shorts – 'is our new PE teacher, Mr Whip.'

I knew it! I knew there was something bad about him! A PE teacher! Of all the teachers in all the schools, PE teachers are the cruellest, and this one looked no different. From the cold, murderous gleam in his eyes, to the cold, hairless look of his legs, I just knew he was going to be a truly evil addition to Little Strangehaven Primary.

'Mr Whip joins us following a celebrated career as a prison officer.'

I think everybody in the hall gulped.

'And next to me,' Dr Errno continued, 'is Ms Stranglebum from Minerva. And they are both here for an exciting announcement!'

Exciting announcements in school were never exciting. They were usually terrible, and I was not wrong here. With a flourish, Dr Errno clicked a clicker and a video started playing on the screen behind him.

It started with the owl logo of Minerva and then flashed up pictures of our school. A smarmy voice spoke over the top.

'It's time for Little Strangehaven to go GREEN! And Minerva Industries are here to help usher in the twenty-first century . . .'

The video cut to Pamela Stranglebum sporting a brilliantly white lab coat. She beamed right down the camera lens.

'After the successful introduction of the robot librarians, the next step in turning Little Strangehaven into the school of the future is the introduction of free renewable energy.'

'That sounds quite good!' I whispered to Agatha.

'Hmm,' Agatha whisper-hmmed, which is actually an incredibly difficult thing to hear and might have just been her normal breathing.

'To achieve this,' video-Stranglebum continued, 'we are rolling out our patented green child-power technology across the whole school.'

I didn't get it. How would painting children green create energy? We had to find out more.

The video ended, and the screen began to rise into the ceiling, revealing a large object hidden under a shiny blanket.

'Now could I please have a volunteer?' Dr Errno asked.

Here was our chance to find out more about this mysterious child-painting technology. My hand shot up.

'Ah!' Dr Errno pointed at me. 'Lennox Tuchus –'

'Yes, Agatha Topps would like to volunteer,' I said.

Agatha shot me a look of stunned admiration for coming up with the idea.

'I think not, Tuchus,' said Dr Errno. 'You just volunteered yourself. Up you come.'

Matzo balls!

I trudged up onstage, nearly tripping over my extra-long new trousers on the way. I paused and gave the whole school a little bow because I was probably a bit of a celebrity in that moment. Once I'd stopped bowing, Dr Errno whipped off the shiny blanket and my bum nearly threw up right there and then when I saw what it had been hiding.

It was a bike.

An exercise bike, but still a bike.

And I couldn't ride a bike. My dad had got me one for my birthday but had always been away, doing important, probably secret-spy-service things, and too busy to teach me. And, because my mum thought there was an ancient bike-riding curse on our family, she never taught me either.

The curse dated back to the nineteenth century,

when my great-great-great-great-grandpa Shlomi Tuchus from Krakow was taking his first-ever bike ride and accidentally ran over a witch. He then panicked and reversed over her, and then panicked some more and rode over her again. The witch was *very* unhappy, and cursed Grandpa Shlomi for evermore. Since then, Tuchuses and bikes have never gone together well.

'Get on, Tuchus,' said Dr Errno.

I felt my knees wobble. 'I can't,' I whispered.

'Get on the bike!'

By now, the whole school was staring, waiting for me to saddle up.

'But I can't ride a bike!' I whisper-wailed to Dr Errno.

'Tuchus. This is an exercise bike. It doesn't move.'

'It's still a bike!'

Mr Whip stalked across the stage and stopped a few millimetres from me. He was so close I could almost taste the oniony scent that was coming off him. I looked up, knees knocking, and said, 'I'm just not very good with bikes. See, there's a family curse –'

But I didn't get to tell Mr Whip about my great-great-great-great-grandpa Shlomi Tuchus and the witch because he blared in my face, 'GET YOUR SCRAWNY BACKSIDE ON THAT BIKE AND START PEDALLING OR ELSE!'

I did not know what *or else* was, but something told me it was probably best not to find out. So I climbed on to the bike and clung to the handlebars for dear life.

Dr Errno said, 'See, now that wasn't so hard, was it?' Then he turned to Pamela Stranglebum, flashed her a smile and said, 'Ms Stranglebum, please continue.'

Pamela Stranglebum stood up and pointed to me with a laser pointer.

'As of today, every child in the school will pedal throughout their lessons. Minerva's patented green child-power technology transforms the pedalling into free energy. There will, of course, be rewards for the best pedallers and repentance tasks for the laziest. We call this initiative Pedal-Power.'

'Get pedalling!' Errno hissed at me.

'I can't –'

'DO IT!'

Whimpering a little, I started pedalling.

'And best of all,' continued Ms Stranglebum, 'the system is completely idiot-proof!'

The wheels began to whiz round and a panel of lights started to glow.

I couldn't believe it! It was working! I was riding. I was *riding* a bike! Finally!

But then the Tuchus family curse came back to haunt me. My overlong new school trousers caught in the gears. There was a terrible ripping sound, a jerking sensation, and then I was flipped head first straight over the handlebars. I soared through the air for what seemed like a very long time and luckily crash-landed on top of some Year Ones at the front of the hall.

'I thought you said it was idiot-proof!' Dr Errno yelped at Pamela Stranglebum.

'It . . . it . . . is!' she said.

It might have been idiot-proof, but it wasn't Tuchus-family-curse-proof.

The whole school was staring at me as I picked myself up. I absolutely was NOT blushing as I walked over and sat back down next to Agatha.

'No sign of any green paint,' I whispered. To which Agatha gave me one of her looks, which was very, very difficult to read.

CHAPTER 2
AGATHA

In the times before the robot librarians, the sight of Lenny catapulting himself off a stationary exercise bike and flying across the school hall, screaming, 'Curse you, Shlomi!' would have resulted in some kind of reaction from us kids. Maybe some gasps, definitely some laughing. We knew better than that now, though.

The owls were always there. Always watching. Always ready to haul you off to a repentance task. I'd been trying to come up with a way to get rid of them, but hearing Pamela Stranglebum's latest plan made me think that those mechanical birds were about to become the least of our worries. I sensed something bigger was afoot and, as I have incredibly powerful spy-detective instincts,

I knew it was best to trust them.

When I was sure the robot owls were circulating at the back of the hall, I leaned towards Lenny and whispered my concerns. He nodded and said, 'Yes, it will be those green children we'll have to keep an eye out for.'

'There aren't any green children,' I said calmly.

I'd been working hard on being more zen around Lenny. He might not be a natural spy-detective, but I could not ignore the fact that he had proven he could be a useful-ish assistant. Sometimes.

'Oh.' He slapped his head. 'By green children, they mean aliens, don't they?' Then he quietly wailed, 'NO, NOT ALIENS! They're the worst!'

I slapped my hand over his mouth and hissed, 'No, not aliens! Lenny, we discussed this: it's *never* aliens. Now, shush. Let's see how this all plays out.'

We turned our attention back to the stage.

'I need another volunteer,' Dr Errno said. 'Who here can actually ride a bike?'

Along with the rest of the school, I stuck my hand up in the air. When spy-detectivizing for clues, it's best to be right in the middle of the action.

But Lenny grabbed my arm and yanked it down. 'No, Agatha! They want to turn you into an alien!'

By the time I'd managed to pull free, Mr Whip was pointing at Ernie, saying, 'I saw that child cycling to school today. He should be able to manage it.'

Ernie stopped chewing on his shoelaces and let out a little whimper.

'Up you come,' Dr Errno said.

Ernie got to his feet and nervously climbed the steps on to the stage. Soon he was pedalling away on the bike, the wheels whizzing round and the panel of lights glowing again.

Pamela Stranglebum stepped forward and dramatically threw her hands upwards. 'Behold! Pedal-Power! Isn't it magnificent?'

'It is!' cried Dr Errno very enthusiastically.

'This boy is the future,' Pamela said, which, no offence to Ernie, didn't sound all *that* promising. I mean, Ernie thinks the number that comes between fourteen and sixteen is fiveteen.

'You are all the future!' Pamela continued, glaring out across the hall. 'Your school will be the first in the world to be powered by sustainable child-power energy.'

Looking at Ernie huffing and puffing, I wasn't sure how sustainable this child-power energy would actually be. He'd already started to slow down, and the light panel was flickering on and off.

Mr Whip strode over and started yelling in his face.

'Come on, boy, put your back into it! Pain is power!'

While Ernie sweated and grunted, and the whole school looked on in stunned silence, Pamela Stranglebum continued.

'When you return to your classrooms, you will find your own individualized-learning Pedal-Pod™. You begin saving the world today!'

Then she laughed. Exactly the kind of evil cackle you would expect from a supervillain.

Dr Errno clapped his hands together and said, 'Now off to class! Let's begin this most wonderful initiative and start the new school year on a high!'

He then turned to Ernie and told him he could stop cycling. Ernie climbed off his bike, then proceeded to weave about the stage on very wobbly legs for a moment before falling flat on his face, groaning about not being able to feel his feet any more.

Dr Errno looked over at Mr Whip and said, 'See to that child.' And then he and Ms Stranglebum stepped over Ernie and headed off in the direction of Dr Errno's office.

Mr Whip nodded curtly, took hold of Ernie's legs and dragged him across the stage. Then he dragged him down the steps, poor Ernie's face bouncing off each and every one. After Mr Whip had dragged Ernie across the length of the hall floor, they disappeared through the double doors, I guess heading to the nurse's room.

The owls then dismissed us, a class at a time, and we all filed out in complete silence and marched in line back to our classrooms. I'm sure everyone's heads were spinning with what we had just witnessed, but nobody dared say anything. Not with the birds about.

Inside the classroom, our desks were nowhere to be seen. In their place was row after row of bikes – just like the one in assembly.

'I don't believe this,' I said. It all just felt . . . wrong.

Miss Happ, who had moved up with us from Year Four, looked down at her tablet and said, as if she was reading from a script, 'Good morning, children. Please mount your Pedal-Pod™ and begin pedalling towards a new greener future.'

Reluctantly, we all got on and began to pedal.

What choice did we have?

Lenny was on the bike next to me. Let's just say he was having some minor difficulties. First attempt, he swung his leg over and ended up sitting on it backwards, then asked me why his bike had no handlebars.

Second go, he jumped on, slipped straight off and landed with one leg either side of the frame. He spent several moments clutching his unmentionables, eyes crossed and whimpering.

Third try, he only got one foot on the pedal, started shouting that his other leg couldn't catch up and gradually slipped to the floor, with one foot still going round.

By this point, Miss Happ had had enough. She said, 'Lennox Tuchus, report down to the Infants. I believe there's a spare Tricycle-Pod there you can use. Can you manage to ride a stationary trike?'

Lenny nodded, but he didn't look that sure.

Miss Happ clapped her hands and an owl

swooped down and hovered next to Lenny, ready to escort him.

I waved him goodbye and focused on my own pedalling. The wheels of my bike began to glow more and more brightly, and I watched my name work its way up past Rahul, then Dipa and Bethany, right to the top of the points leader board at the front of the class. I imagined going home and telling my parents that I'd done the best, and how

proud they'd be. That they might actually take a moment to notice me.

I saw Jordan glance over at me, then back at the leader board. He narrowed his eyes and began pedalling faster, so I upped my own pace a little. That top spot was mine.

Miss Happ began our lesson on expanded noun phrases and we all typed our work into the computer screens mounted on the handlebars of each of our Pedal-Pods™.

Really, I should have continued trying to work out what was going on with all the Minerva technology that was creeping into our school, but instead I found myself focusing more and more on earning points for my pedalling. They were racking up. My light bar on the leader board kept growing and growing, and, every time I reached a new level, a nice-sounding lady voice said, 'Well done, Agatha. You are fantastic. The rest of the class have nothing on you! Keep pedalling!'

So I did. Because who doesn't like to be told that they're fantastic?

CHAPTER 3

LENNY

I trudged down to the Infants, feeling very cross about great-great-great-great-grandpa Shlomi Tuchus and the fact that Dad had never taught me to ride a bike.

I turned the corner and standing there in his tiny shorts was Mr Whip.

'You there!' He pointed at me. 'What are you doing out of class?'

I told him how I'd been sent to get a tricycle from the Infants' room.

'Ah, that's right,' Mr Whip sneered. 'You're the boy who can't ride a bike, aren't you?' I nodded.

He bent down and put his nose right up to mine.

'I don't like children who aren't good at sport. You do . . . like sport, don't you?'

I swallowed nervously and nodded.

'Good. Well, I'll be keeping a VERY close eye on you in PE lessons. Now run along.'

I started running away from Mr Whip as fast as possible, but unfortunately my too-long trousers tripped me, and I went sprawling. I looked back, and Mr Whip glared at me, pointed at his eyes, then pointed at me.

I'm watching you, he mouthed.

Ugh. PE teachers.

A moment later, I knocked on the door of the Infant class.

Miss Buttercup waved me in. All the children were panting and puffing as they pedalled away, while answering questions on their number bonds to ten.

'Now what can I do for you, young man?' Miss Buttercup asked with a warm smile. Miss Buttercup was the nicest teacher in the school, and her smile made me feel a bit funny in the knees.

'I need to trick up a pycicle, Miss Cutterbup,' I said.

As soon as the words came out, I knew they weren't quite right. There was something about Miss Buttercup that made me forget how to speak, but remember how to blush.

Miss Buttercup gave me another smile, and told me to pick a trike up from the back of the class.

One of the children, a girl with glasses and bunches, pointed at me and said, 'You're the one who fell off the bike in assembly!'

I blushed even more furiously. 'My trousers got caught in the gears, OK?!' I snapped. 'It could have happened to anyone!'

I turned to Miss Buttercup, who gave me a look of sympathy, as if I was a puppy who had just fallen head first into its water bowl.

'Yeah,' said the girl. 'Anyone who's a big, clumsy dunderhead!'

It was because I didn't want Miss Buttercup to think I was a big, clumsy dunderhead that I said what I said next, I suppose. I wanted her to look at me with admiration in her eyes, not pity.

'YEAH, WELL, ACTUALLY I'M NOT A BIG, CLUMSY DUNDERHEAD AND LAST TERM I ACTUALLY SAVED THIS SCHOOL AND THE WHOLE WORLD! I was ACTUALLY incredibly brave and had to fight warrior chickens and child-eating Transylvanian gargoyles and deadly toilet-paper mummies and I nearly floated into space and then I almost got choked by my own underpants before I could stop the old librarian, Mr Pardon, using a book to destroy everything, but I did a flying kick through the air and he got sucked into the *Book of Chaos*, which was actually a talking book, and it flipped shut and I saved the day!'

Silence fell over the class, a sort of hushed awe at the magnitude of what I had achieved.

I turned to look at Miss Buttercup. But instead of admiration in her eyes there was . . . concern.

'Are you feeling OK, Lenny?' she asked gently.

'Yes, why?' I said, confused.

'You were . . . choked by your own underpants?'

'Yes!' I nodded, putting on my best heroic face and staring off into the distance like soldiers do in war films. 'But I'm fine now, thanks for asking.'

My heart swelled because now Miss Buttercup knew how brave I was AND she cared.

'*Riiiiiight,*' said Miss Buttercup. 'Do you need to visit the school nurse, Lenny?'

Wow. She *really* cared.

'No, honestly,' I said. 'The killer wedgie was ages ago and I'm OK.'

I gave her a wink, which I'm still not great at, so I had to use both eyes.

I went to the back of the class, grabbed a tricycle Pedal-Pod™ that wasn't being used, and dragged it across the room. I stopped at the door and gave Miss Buttercup a proud salute, and she stared at me, open-mouthed, clearly super impressed. In fact, she was so bowled over by my heroism she couldn't find the words to say anything.

A few moments later, I had dragged the tricycle back to my classroom, and plugged it in next to Agatha. She was pedalling furiously, sweat beading on her brow.

'Can't . . . talk . . . now,' she panted. 'Top of . . . leader board.'

Indeed, there she was in first place, two points ahead of Jordan Wiener, son of the school cleaner, who was also pedalling furiously and so red in the face he looked like a very determined tomato.

I scanned the leader board. I was second bottom with only two points! The only person below me was Ernie, who had minus twenty-seven.

He had been pedalling backwards all morning and had somehow actually sucked power *out* of the school.

I hopped on my tricycle perfectly and started pedalling. Ten minutes later, Agatha whispered to me.

'Your score hasn't gone up much!'

I looked at the leader board. She was right. My score had only risen one point since I started, but Agatha's had gone up four. My numbers were creeping up way slower than everybody else's!

'It's because this trike has smaller wheels!' I said.

'You're sure it's not because you're pedalling slower?' she asked.

Er, *rude*!

'No! It must be the wheels!' I gasped.

Worse still, it looked like Ernie had worked out how to pedal forwards now and was quickly catching up to my score. I *couldn't* be last in the class, and, if my huge physical efforts were being scuppered by my tiny wheels, I had to use my huge brain to keep ahead. The leader board said we'd be awarded bonus points for exceptional work or giving answers in class, and I was certain I was more exceptional than Ernie, who last year had managed to staple his test papers to his hand THREE TIMES.

I, on the other hand, had worked out how not to staple a test paper to my hand after the first time I did it. But then I've always been a quick learner.

It was going to be a battle of wits against Ernie.

I just had to concentrate and win some extra points through my exceptionalitiness.

The opportunity came later that afternoon. Ernie was pedalling well, but he had lost a point for saying that the capital of France was 'a big letter F' and then at break he had accidentally sat on Miss Happ's chocolate éclair (the big, creamy sort, not the little sweet) and was docked another. Now we were in an RE lesson, talking about all the different religions. Ernie was still only three points behind me, but I had a cunning plan.

When nobody was looking, I quietly passed him two pieces of paper, and a stapler.

A moment later, I heard a yelp from behind me. Ernie was flapping his hand wildly in the air, the paper stapled to it.

He lost two more points for that, and my position in second-bottom place felt a little more secure.

CHAPTER 4

AGATHA

I felt a bit sorry for Lenny for two reasons. Well, several reasons actually, but let's focus on the ones that were most pressing at the time:

1. Somebody really should have taught him how to ride a bike.

2. The trike was way too small for him. He looked like Donkey Kong sitting on his little go-kart. *And* he was still having major problems pedalling the thing. Until I told him to look forward and not down, he was kneeing himself in the face every time the pedals went round.

Surprisingly, though, Lenny seemed delighted with his performance. As we walked out of the classroom at the end of the lesson, he said, 'I think we can chalk that up as a pretty successful day so far.'

I came to an abrupt halt and said, '*What*?' because he literally had fourteen points.

'Yup, pleased with that result. I think we can agree that I smashed it in the end, thanks to my exceptionalistic brainpower.'

'Lenny, my score stands at four hundred and sixty-three.'

'What's your point?'

'What's my point? You're on a score of fourteen, Lenny. No offence or anything, but I wouldn't say you were smashing it. If anybody is smashing it, it's me.'

He glared at me for a moment, then said quite rudely, 'Well, thank you, Agatha. Here's *my* point for you to wrap your ears round. No, make that *points* – I actually have many points for you to listen to.'

He held a defiant-looking finger up to my face.

'Point number one: saying "no offence" does not mean that the thing you say next is not offensive.'

He stuck up two more fingers.

'Point number two: nobody likes a show-off, *Little-Miss-I've-Got-Sixteen-Thousand-Billion-and Eleventeen-Hundred-Points*.'

He held up three more fingers.

'And point number three: your points were just earned by your knees. Whereas all fourteen of *my* points have been earned through the very incredibleness and exceptionalitivity of my brain. And a stapler.'

'Lenny.'

'Yes?'

'You've made three points, but you're holding six fingers up.'

He looked at them, tilted his head, and eventually put two fingers down.

'Better?'

'Oooh . . . so close.'

I waited as he looked up to the ceiling and did some mental maths and then, finally, and with a very unwarranted triumphant nod, lowered one more finger.

'And another thing,' I continued, 'how were my points only earned by my knees?'

'Duh!' he said. 'That's how you cycle – using your knees.'

'OK, there's some other bits involved too, like your feet and your hamstrings and the quadriceps.'

'What have dinosaurs got to do with cycling?'

'Lenny, *literally what*?'

He threw his hands in the air. 'You're the one who brought up quadriceps! And I don't want to argue with you about stupid pedalling points!'

I didn't want to argue with him either. 'I'm sorry,' I said. 'You're right. It was just nice to be noticed for doing well at something, that's all.'

'You're kidding!' Lenny said. 'You do great at everything! Everyone notices that!'

'Not everyone,' I said quietly, and, before he could say any more, I changed the subject. The pedalling had distracted me for a few hours, but Minerva still needed investigating. 'Anyway, I want to have a chat with Gregor and find out if he saw anything over the summer holidays.'

'You mean the Scottish gargoyle that the *Book of Chaos* brought to life last term? The one who lives in the school attic, which is why he might have spotted any suspicious Minerva activity over the holidays?'

'Lenny, why are you telling me this? I know who Gregor is.'

'Just saying it in case anybody has forgotten. Or doesn't know who Gregor is.'

'Anybody *who*? It's only me here!'

'You never know who might be watching or listening, Agatha,' Lenny said in a weirdly mysterious voice.

I rolled my eyes and decided not to ask him anything else. I didn't want to encourage him. I looked around to check there weren't any owls flapping about. The coast was clear, but I lowered my voice just to be safe.

'Minerva being back in school is something we should investigate. I want to find out if it really is a green-energy initiative.'

'Because . . .?' Lenny said.

'Because we are spy-detectives, Lennox! We

find things out! And, besides, don't you have a feeling?'

Lenny's eyeballs did a couple of big circles in their sockets like he was trying to figure out whether he had a feeling or not. I wasn't convinced he did, but he said, 'Yes, I have a feeling. A very spy-detectory feeling.'

'I just think the school is . . . changing. And maybe not in a good way,' I continued. 'Little Strangehaven Primary used to be a happy place, but then the owls came in with their boring books and repentance tasks, and all the fun and laughter just stopped. And now this pedalling . . . I mean, I can handle it, but did you see some of the other kids? People were falling asleep in their sponge and custard at lunch because they were so tired. Did you notice poor Ernie? He comfort-sucked his way through two entire Pritt Sticks this afternoon. That's a lot of glue, even for him.'

Lenny nodded. 'You know what, Agatha? I think there is something going on at Little

Strangehaven and that we need to take a closer look at Minerva. We should ask Gregor if he spotted anything strange over the holidays. Now have you finished prattling on about dinosaurs so we can get on with my very important spy-detective mission?'

I opened my mouth and shut it a few times because I could not believe what I was hearing.

'Agatha, is there something wrong with your mouth?'

'No, Lenny! There's nothing wrong with my mouth!'

He started up the staircase that led to the roof. 'Well, let's get going then! What are you waiting for?'

Be zen, Agatha. He's a useful assistant sometimes, I reminded myself as I started my deep-breathing exercises and tried to picture a field of buttercups. *Useful-ish . . .*

CHAPTER 5

LENNY

If you'd told me just a few months ago that I'd be going up to the school attic to see a walking, talking, real-life Scottish stone gargoyle, I might not have believed you. I mean, I *might* have done. Who's to say what is real? Grandpa Joseph used to tell me stories about how his garden gnomes would come alive and creep into the house at night and drink all his whisky. I never believed him, but perhaps he was telling the truth after all?

The point is nobody knows. And there I was, talking to an actual gargoyle in the huge, dusty attic directly under the school roof. Gregor had let us in after we'd given the secret knock on the door.

'Gregor, do gnomes exist?'

'Aye,' said Gregor, nibbling on a brick, his

scrunched-up face scrunching even more in what I think was a look of disgust. 'They do – and right pains in the bahookie they are too! Stealin' all the good whisky – no wonder they have such jolly wee faces! If I can give ye one word of advice in life, laddie, it's never, ever, EVER trust a gnome.'

'What about fairies? Do they exist?'

'Fairies? Have ye gone soft in the head? Of course they dinnae exist! Ha! Wha' next? Ye'll be believin' dragons exist! Or kangaroos!'

'Kangaroos do exist,' I said, but for a moment he had me doubting myself.

'Och aye, course they do!' Gregor roared, and slapped his bony legs. 'Bouncin' aboot the place and boxin'! Pull the other one – it's go' bells on!' He started hopping about the attic. 'Look at me! I'm a kangaroo!'

Agatha, who had her hands on her hips, snapped, 'Can you STOP that? You're making a racket and we are TRYING to keep you a secret!'

Gregor stopped jumping immediately, looking nervously at Agatha.

'Now,' she sighed, 'can we *please* focus?'

'You should definitely focus,' I warned Gregor.

'Aye, yer right there, laddie. Best we stop bletherin'. She has that face on her like a slapped bahookie, which means –'

'WHICH MEANS I WILL THROTTLE YOU BOTH IF I DON'T GET SILENCE!'

Both Gregor and I decided that silence was the

best course of action. Having been recently throttled by both a toilet-paper mummy and my own underpants, I did not want any more throat trauma.

Agatha closed her eyes and rubbed the bridge of her nose for quite a long time while Gregor and I exchanged shrugs.

'Right, that's better,' she said eventually. 'Now, Gregor, we came up here to find out if you had seen anything suspicious over the holidays. Minerva and Ms Stranglebum are back in the school with these new energy-generating pedalling machines, and my spy-detective instincts are telling me something strange might be going on.'

Gregor stood in silence, not moving a muscle.

'So,' continued Agatha, 'have you seen anything . . . unusual?'

Gregor stood in even more silence, still not moving a muscle. He was almost like a statue again.

'Gregor,' Agatha said through gritted teeth, 'you can speak again now.'

'Och right. I didnae want to take any chances.'

'*Just. Answer. The. Question*,' said Agatha.

I couldn't help notice that her hands had balled into fists. I edged backwards slightly.

'Well, lassie,' said Gregor, 'now that ye mention it, I did indeed see some shifty shenanigans over the summer. There were people toing and froing from the basement wi' all sorts o' curious-looking equipment. Enormous oojamaflaps and whackin' great thingamajigs, they were. That was followed by strange hummin' noises and the lights flickerin' on and off. All very curious.'

'That sounds like it needs investigating!' Agatha said and clapped her hands together decisively.

'Yes,' I said, and clapped twice to show I was even more decisive. 'We should definitely sneak past the deadly robot owls with their all-seeing eyes and investigate the creepy basement. That sounds like a brilliant idea. Actually, now that I think about it, *is* it a brilliant idea?'

Agatha tutted me, then said, 'Thanks, Gregor! You've actually been useful!'

'At yer service,' he said and gave a little bow. While he was bent over, he picked up another brick and started chewing on it.

We clambered through the attic door, and hopped down the stairs. Suddenly out from behind the corner jumped Jordan Wiener and his sticky-up hair.

'Ha ha!' he ha-ha'd.

'Ha?' I said, not sure what else to say.

'I knew you two were up to something! What were you doing in the attic? That's out of bounds.'

'We weren't up to anything. And if I were you,' Agatha said, shoving her face in Jordan's, which was difficult because he was a head taller than her, 'I'd keep your nose right out of it.'

Jordan Wiener took a nervous step back, and I don't blame him. I'm probably the bravest boy in the school, but even I wouldn't want to get on the wrong side of Agatha Topps.

'Well . . .' said Jordan, backing even further away, 'I know you're up to something. You and that grey monster-thing that nobody else believes exists, but definitely *does* exist because last term it punched me right on the nose for no reason! I'm watching you!' he said, then ran away.

'We're going to have to do something about him,' Agatha said with a terrible dark look in her eyes.

I gulped. 'No! Agatha! We *cannot* kill Jordan. Somebody might notice!'

'Lennox Tuchus! That is not what I meant. We need to convince him he made a mistake about seeing Gregor. And someone noticing is not the reason why I'm not killing him. I'm not killing him because killing is wrong. Even when it comes to Jordan Wiener.'

We arrived back in our room just in time for the last class of the day.

I got back on my trike and started pedalling,

the numbers on the leader board creeping up – Agatha in the lead, just ahead of Jordan; me second-bottom, just ahead of Ernie. A moment later, I was a bit further ahead because in our maths lesson on 2D shapes he said that a polygon was a missing parrot.

While Miss Happ was trying to explain that polygons had nothing to do with jungle birds, the door opened and Ms Stranglebum and Mr Whip strode in. Agatha and I glanced at each other as Mr Whip weaved through the bikes, ordering kids to pedal faster and generally being menacing and quite prison-wardeny. Ms Stranglebum had a whispery-conversation with Miss Happ, but we couldn't hear what they were saying over the sound of the bikes, and we didn't dare stop in case we dropped down the leader board.

Finally, Miss Happ held her hand up for us all to stop cycling, which I did happily because my legs were jellified, but I think Agatha kept pedalling for a bit longer.

'Could Ernie Strewdel please accompany Ms Stranglebum and Mr Whip to the . . .?'

Miss Happ left her unfinished sentence hanging in mid-air, but neither Ms Stranglebum nor Mr Whip finished it.

Ernie looked at Miss Happ blankly.

'Come on, Ernie!' Miss Happ said. 'Ms Stranglebum and Mr Whip don't have all day!'

Ernie clambered off his bike, and reluctantly walked up to the front of the class. Ms Stranglebum gave him a cold smile, and Mr Whip put his hand firmly on Ernie's shoulder and steered him out of the room. Ernie gave a little whimper and shot a forlorn look back at us as he was frogmarched through the door.

Agatha's hand shot straight up. 'Miss, why is Ernie going with Mr Whip and Ms Stranglebum?'

'I'm not quite sure. He's . . . erm . . . just running some errands for them, I expect,' Miss Happ said vaguely.

'What sort of errands?' asked Agatha.

'That's none of your business, young lady! Now, everybody, get cycling!'

Agatha didn't need to be told a second time, and started pedalling fiercely, but not before she gave me a curious look.

A look that said mystery.

A look that said danger.

Or a look that said she needed the toilet – I wasn't completely sure, if I'm honest, so I just gave her one of my winning smiles back, followed up with a double eye-wink, just for good measure.

CHAPTER 6

AGATHA

I think I wondered about Ernie for all of two seconds after Ms Stranglebum and Mr Whip took him away because I quickly refocused on answering maths questions while pedalling as powerfully as possible. I wanted more points. I *needed* more points. I was definitely pulling away from Jordan. I glanced at the clock. It was almost the end of the day – there was no way he'd catch me now.

Lenny was still languishing near the bottom of the leader board. He didn't help himself, though. Despite Miss Happ having clearly told Ernie after the polygon incident that 2D shapes weren't anything to do with animals, Lenny had still claimed that an octagon was a lost octopus and a nonagon was a missing grandmother.

When the clock stuck half past three, a loud klaxon sounded, which was a surprise. So much of a surprise to Lenny that he screamed and kneed himself in the face again.

Miss Happ clapped her hands together. 'Please stop cycling! The end-of-day klaxon has sounded.'

The leader board at the front of the classroom flashed all the colours of the rainbow, which made everybody do an impressed *Oooooh!*, and

JTING HIGHE

the words **COMPUTING HIGHEST SCORER** scrolled across the screen.

While my classmates all draped themselves over their handlebars, trying to catch their breath, I kept my eyes pinned to the screen, imagining my parents' proud faces when I told them I'd won.

'Where did I come? Where did I come? Did I win?!' I heard somebody shout, and was surprised that the somebody was me.

It is possible that my overcompetitiveness had leaked out of me in a moment of excited apprehension.

A message flashed up.

TODAY LITTLE STRANGEHAVEN PRIMARY HAS CREATED ENOUGH GREEN ENERGY TO POWER THE SCHOOL FOR TWO DAYS.

Nice – but what was my final score?

THROUGH YOUR EFFORTS, YOU HAVE PREVENTED FIFTEEN SQUARE CENTIMETRES OF POLAR ICE CAP

FROM MELTING.

Not bad either, but where were the results?

YOU HAVE STOPPED THE DEFORES-TATION OF AN AREA OF RAINFOREST THE SIZE OF A DOORMAT.

All right already, I got it – we'd been very green, but who had come top?!

'That will make those missing parrots happy,' Lenny said. I ignored him.

YOU HAVE SAVED A FAMILY OF BLUE-FOOTED BOOBIES FROM BEING EVICTED FROM THEIR HOME.

'OH, FOR GOODNESS' SAKE!' I shouted. 'I don't care about the blue-footed booby, or the rainforest, or the ice caps! *Just tell me if I won!*'

'Agatha!' Lenny said, clearly horrified. 'You don't care about the blue-footed booby?'

'I-I . . . do. Sorry, that came out wrong,' I stammered, shrinking a little and embarrassed by my outburst. 'I'm just keen to know how we all did.'

I was pretty sure I'd earned the most points in

the class. But had I done the best out of the whole school? It would be something to have beaten the Year Sixes!

'Any moment now,' Miss Happ said, giving me a disapproving look. She was obviously a fan of the blue-footed booby too.

A happy little jingle played and then *finally* the Little Strangehaven Primary Top Ten appeared.

'Hey, Agatha,' Lenny said. 'You came fourth out of the whole school! That's amazing!'

Fourth. It wasn't bad, I supposed. But it wasn't *first* and I couldn't help but feel disappointed.

'Well done, Agatha Topps,' Miss Happ said, giving me a big smile. 'Top of the class, narrowly beating Jordan!'

'Would we say *narrowly*?' I replied. 'I think the word you mean is *convincingly*.'

Jordan gave me a glare, which I enjoyed and beamed back at him.

Miss Happ picked up a Minerva Pedal-Power information booklet and started reading. 'Your scores will be added together each day and children can earn prizes by getting the most points at the end of every half-term.'

'Prizes?' Jordan said. 'Like what?'

'You get to wear a special blazer; you'll be allowed in special areas of the school . . .'

Excitement rippled through the classroom. A special blazer! Special areas!

'You also get to skip the lunch queue, have extra helpings, and you'll be assigned your own underling to fetch and carry things for you –'

'Underling? What's an underling?' Lenny asked. He was holding on to his handlebars tightly, I think to stop him slipping off his trike.

I didn't know what an underling was either, but I had a feeling I wanted one!

'It means that students who fall below the line of satisfactory output will work for the top points earners.'

'I don't think the name "underling" is very flattering, Miss Happ,' Lenny said.

'I don't imagine it's meant to be, Lennox. And, with your score of thirty-eight points today, I'm afraid it's looking likely that you'll become one.'

'What?' Lenny slammed his fists down, stood up on his pedals, then sort of fell back off his trike. The wheels spun backwards one complete revolution.

'Make that thirty-seven points, Lennox,' Miss Happ said.

'But I don't want to be an underling! I am not underling material! I'm more of an . . . overling!' Lenny said, then stood up, banged his head on his handlebars, and fell back down again.

Miss Happ folded her arms. 'As I said, underlings won't be assigned until the end of the first half-term. Perhaps tomorrow might be a more successful day for you.'

Her tone of voice did not suggest that she thought this would be true.

I felt sorry for Lenny. Again. But that wasn't what I was really focusing on.

I was focusing on those privileges and thinking about being *special*. I had already made a promise in my head that the next day it would be me in first place. I'd be the best in the school and earn a gazillion points. I'd get that special blazer and a whole load of Lennys – oops, I mean *underlings* – to carry my bags for me.

Looking back, I think this might have been the point where I kind of lost myself in the Pedal-Power propaganda machine. What can I say? I've always been very rewards driven. How do you know you're worth anything if you don't have the prizes to prove it?

'This Pedal-Power initiative is awesome!' I said to Lenny as we headed out of the school gate at the end of the day. While I was striding with the determination of someone who would stop at nothing to be the best, he was waddling along a bit like a duck – I think he might have been slightly saddle-sore.

'I'm getting an early night,' I said, 'so I'm well rested and raring to take the top spot tomorrow.'

'Is it awesome, though, Agatha?' Lenny said doubtfully as he rubbed his bum. 'I know we're doing it to save the environment –'

'Are we?' I said.

'Yes, Agatha, we are pedalling for a greener future,' Lenny said.

'Well, one of us is,' I said under my breath. Honestly, if it was down to Lenny on his trike, those blue-footed boobies wouldn't stand a chance.

'But remember you said your spy-detective instincts were telling you something strange was going on,' Lenny continued. 'I think you were right. I don't like this cycling malarkey at all.'

I waved my hand dismissively. 'Ah, I think I overreacted. It's fine. You know, I think I'm going to wear my trainers tomorrow, and some stretchy leggings instead of my school trousers.'

'Agatha,' Lenny said, 'we need to get spy-detectory all over Minerva ASAP!'

'Lenny, just because you're at the bottom of the leader board doesn't mean something weird is going on! That's the only reason you want to investigate – because I'm clearly doing so much better than you.'

'It's not because of that!' Lenny said, looking wounded – which I feel completely horrible about now, but didn't really at the time. 'And having more points doesn't mean you're better than me.'

'It kind of does,' I said. But I was wrong about that. I was wrong about a lot of things.

'But Gregor saw weird oojamaflaps going on in the summer. And where did that Stranglebum woman take Ernie? Did you notice he never came back to class?'

I had, but I wasn't really interested, so I said, 'Do you think if I stuff a spare jumper in my leggings it would be the same as those padded shorts professional cyclists wear?'

'Agatha!' Lenny shouted. 'You're not listening! I said Ernie never came back.'

I slung my arm over Lenny's shoulder and we started off down the road. 'Chill out, Lenny. You know what Ernie's like. He probably made an excuse because he didn't want to come back and pedal. He always tries to get out of PE. Remember that time he got his head stuck in a trombone on purpose, so he didn't have to do cross-country?'

'Well, he'd better be in class tomorrow,' Lenny said. 'He's the only thing keeping me off the bottom of the leader board. I don't want to be an underling.' Then, very quietly, he said, 'Agatha, please will you teach me to ride a bike?'

I didn't notice the desperation in Lenny's eyes. I didn't pick up on the deep sadness in his voice. I was too busy thinking about all the privileges and glory I would get when I was number one on the leader board. So, instead of saying to my best friend in the whole world that of course I'd help him learn to ride a bike, I said, 'Do you think the special blazers will have special badges on them?'

When I got home, I was excited to tell Mum and Dad how well I'd done. As I walked through the front door, I shouted, 'I have news!'

'In here!' Dad called back.

I went into the sitting room and found my whole family: Mum and Dad; the twin babies, Trevor and Nigel; Mavis and Iris, my younger sisters; and George and Tom, my other brothers.

'Agatha! Watch this!' Dad shouted as Trevor and Nigel toddled across the carpet. 'Look at them go!'

'They're walking!' Mum said, swooping them into a hug and kissing them on their heads. 'Aren't they clever?'

'But look! I can do a forward roll!' Mavis said,

and curled into a ball and flapped about on the floor for a bit like an upturned tortoise.

Then Iris started singing some song she'd learned, and George and Tom jumped up and re-enacted a goal they'd scored at football club, using a cushion for the ball.

Dad clapped his hands together and said, 'Well, aren't I blessed with a talented family! I couldn't be more proud!' Then he turned to me and said,

'Agatha, what's your news?'

I didn't really feel like telling him, not after everyone else's performances, but I said, 'I came fourth in this new pedalling thing at school.'

'Fourth is nothing to be disappointed about!' he said, rubbing me on the head.

'As long as you try, Agatha, that's all that matters,' Mum said. Then she turned to Dad as Trevor and Nigel stumbled off again. 'Go and get your phone, quick! We need to film this!'

'I'm going to work really hard and get first place!' I called after Dad.

'Wonderful, darling,' Mum said, her eyes fixed on my brothers.

No one noticed as I slipped out of the sitting room. I went up to my bedroom and lay down on the bed, and I made a promise to myself that I'd get to the top of that leader board and make Mum and Dad notice me.

CHAPTER 7
LENNY

I slammed the door when I got home because slamming doors always makes me feel better and is an easier way to announce that you're in a bad mood than saying, 'Hi, Mum, I had a rubbish day at school because I asked my best friend for help and she ignored me.'

I'm not suggesting that telling Mum that would make me start crying, but why take the risk?

I could hear her talking on the phone to Dad, and that gave me an idea. I rushed into the lounge.

'Mum, can I have a word with Dad?'

I held my hand out for the phone and she passed it to me.

'Hi, Lenny,' my dad said. 'How are –'

'Hi, Dad. Can you come and visit and teach me

to ride a bike, please?'

There was the longest pause. Then, 'Course I can, son. As soon as possible.'

Everything was always 'as soon as possible' with my dad. I'm not sure he actually understood what 'soon' meant.

'When's that *exactly*?' I asked.

'Well,' he said, 'I've got a bit more work to do over the next few days, then I'll come and take you out and we'll get you cycling, no bother!'

I knew that with dad a few days could mean anything from four to six weeks. Sometimes it was hard being the son of an international spy.

'I've just got to go to this blasted conference in Hull,' he said.

Did spies go to conferences in Hull? Probably not. It sounded like exactly the sort of cover a really clever secret agent would use!

'OK, Dad, see you soon then.' I tried to keep my voice happy, but I couldn't help but let a bit of sadness accidentally slip in.

After the phone call, my mum gave me one of those adult smiles that are more like an apology than a smile.

'You know I'd help you if I knew how to ride a bike. But, from the email the school sent about this Pedal-Power initiative, I'm sure you'll learn in no time. It's all very good, isn't it – cycling to save the planet? My little green hero!' She ruffled my hair and went off to cook dinner.

When I got into bed that night, thoughts of tricycles and Minerva wheeled around in my head. There was definitely something suspicious going on. As I couldn't sleep, I decided to do a spot of spy-detective work all on my own. I turned on my laptop and typed Minerva Industries into the search engine. Lots of links came up to their home page, plastered with Pamela Stranglebum's smiling face. I couldn't find anything about Pedal-Power, though. Maybe because it was a new thing?

Then I spotted a link to a report. I clicked on it

and it brought up an official-looking document that said, MINERVA INDUSTRIES FINED FOR ENVIRONMENTAL DAMAGES. Toxic fumes and poisonous waste reach dangerous levels at Minerva facility.

Interesting. It didn't sound like Minerva was that green after all. I jumped back into bed and switched off my light. I'd tell Agatha first thing in the morning.

The next day, I waddled to school, my bum still sore from all the cycling the day before. I walked into class just as the klaxon sounded. Agatha was already there, poised on her Pedal-Pod™. I winced as I climbed on to the saddle of my trike, then whispered, 'I have important spy-detective information. Minerva has been in trouble for environmental violations.'

Agatha frowned, then shrugged. 'Maybe that's why Ms Stranglebum is introducing Pedal-Power. To make amends?'

I didn't think that seemed likely, but I couldn't tell Agatha because a robot owl had swooped in to hover over our heads.

'Commence cycling, Lennox,' Miss Happ said. 'You don't want to get left behind again.'

My already weary legs began to pedal.

'Now that I have your attention,' Miss Happ said, 'I can tell you about a very exciting school trip we have planned next week!'

An exciting school trip! My heart leaped a little. Maybe we were off to the water park! Or Adventureland! I'd always wanted to ride on the Vomit Comet rollercoaster!

'We will be going to Little Strangehaven Museum!'

I groaned inwardly. Teachers must live very boring lives if they think museums are exciting.

'We'll get to see exhibits on medieval Britain and Roman artefacts, as well as the world's largest and most valuable ruby, which is travelling all the way here from Kathmandu via Crawley!' Miss Happ said excitedly.

She could sound excited all she liked. A giant ruby was hardly the same as a rollercoaster that had made one kid puke out of his eyeballs.

'Now, pedal on! We have mathematics to get through!'

After about twenty minutes of hard pedalling and even harder maths, I nodded to the empty bike next to me. 'Ernie's still not back!' I panted at Agatha.

He was bottom of the leader board with no points – mostly because he wasn't around to get any, allowing me to streak into a twelve-point lead. My position at second-bottom looked secure for another day. Hooray for me! But I couldn't shake the feeling that it was a bit weird that he'd been taken out of class yesterday and not returned. What had Pamela Stranglebum and Mr Whip wanted with Ernie anyway?

'Probably off sick,' Agatha said, not sounding that interested.

I frowned. As much as I liked the safety of my nearly-thirteen-point lead, I was worried about Ernie. And that afternoon I only got worrieder.

We were in the middle of a lesson on Vikings when the door burst open and in strutted Ernie Strewdel. Now the first odd thing was that Ernie had never strutted before in his life. He shuffled or stumbled, sometimes tottered, but Ernie did NOT strut. And yet here he was, swaggering towards his bike.

The next odd thing was that Ernie was wearing head-to-toe Lycra with the Minerva logo emblazoned on the front. He even had a cycle helmet on his head – a proper pointy racing one. Again, Ernie was not the Lycra or snazzy helmet wearing type. He wore a parka in summer, and the only hat I'd ever seen him wear was of the bobbled variety.

The *next* odd thing was that he hopped on to his Pedal-Pod™ and started pedalling so fast I saw smoke coming out of the wheels. It was unbelievable! Within a few moments, he had overtaken me on the leader board. I was both impressed and outraged!

But none of this was as odd as what happened next. It started with Miss Happ asking if anybody knew where Vikings came from.

Ernie's hand shot up. Miss Happ sighed, but nodded at him.

'Vikings,' said Ernie, 'often known as Norsemen or Northmen, came from Scandinavia, originating from the area that has become modern-day Denmark, Sweden and Norway. These pagan warriors colonized large areas of Europe during the ninth to eleventh centuries and had a profound influence on the prevailing culture of the time.'

The whole class stared at Ernie. I stared at Ernie and then at Agatha, who stared back at me in disbelief. Even Miss Happ gawped at Ernie. Basically, everybody was staring everywhere, apart from Ernie who just kept on pedalling at a blinding rate.

'Bonus ten points to . . . Ernie,' Miss Happ stammered. That took Ernie to halfway up the leader board already.

I was in last place. What evil trickery was afoot?

It got even worse in English. We were reading

Frankenstein, and Miss Happ asked if we should feel sorry for the monster. Ernie's hand shot up.

'Yes,' he said. 'The creature's monstrosity results only from his grotesque appearance and the unnatural manner of his creation. One can argue that the ambition and selfishness of his creator, Victor Frankenstein, show him to be the true monster.'

Let me be clear – the day before, Ernie had thought that a noun was a religious woman in a long black dress.

Clearly startled at Ernie's newfound brainpower, Miss Happ started testing him.

'What's the capital of Namibia?'

'Windhoek.'

'What's the chemical symbol for copper?'

'Cu.'

'Who's bottom of the leader board now Ernie has become mysteriously clever overnight?'

'Lenny Tuchus.'

OK, that question wasn't actually asked, but it

was the right answer. I was bottom of the leader board.

And that was very not fair.

'There's something fishy going on here, Agatha,' I said, getting hotter inside and out. 'And it needs investigating! Ernie's some sort of mastermind, I don't think Minerva is green at all, and where is all this power we're making really going?'

Agatha didn't even look at me. 'Stop complaining! Just pedal harder!'

She didn't seem to want to discuss it. That was until, five minutes before the end of the day, Ernie overtook her and claimed first place on the leader board.

'There's something very fishy going on here, Lenny,' Agatha said, fuming. 'And it needs investigating!'

CHAPTER 8
AGATHA

I admit I didn't take losing to Ernie that brilliantly. I just couldn't understand it. He'd started after me, and, well, it was Ernie. In a battle of muscle and brains, there was no way he should have ended up ahead. *Something* had to be going on, and, as it was affecting me, I was going to get to the bottom of it.

After we had been dismissed at the end of the day, I bolted after Ernie and caught up with him in the corridor.

'Oi, Ernie!' I shouted.

'Ah, Agatha,' he said, spinning round and giving me a big smile. 'Valiant effort today!'

Valiant effort? Since when did Ernie speak like that? I stared at him hard. Who even was he?

'You did very well,' he continued and patted my shoulder, which I DID NOT appreciate.

'But *you* won!' I spluttered. 'How did you win? I wanted to win! It should have been *meeeee*!'

'I think the real winner is the environment, Agatha,' Ernie replied.

'The environment doesn't get a special blazer!' I shouted back. 'Or a Lenny – I mean an underling – to carry their stuff!'

It was at this point that Lenny appeared, ziggle-zaggling towards us on his wibbly-wobbly legs. He bounced off one set of lockers, then careered into the water fountain, then knocked the fire extinguisher off the wall.

'My legs are very, completely exhausted,' he said. 'How did you do it, Ern? Get so pedallingly powerful and so clever so fast? What happened to you?'

Ernie shrugged. 'I trained and I studied.'

'You trained and you studied?' I spluttered. 'There's no way you could do enough training in one night to do what you just did!'

'It would appear that I did,' Ernie said calmly.

'You must have cheated! Your Pedal-Pod™ had some kind of motor installed or something. Didn't it? Didn't it?!' I gabbled, grabbing the stretchy Lycra of his racing vest, then pinging it back on him.

'I didn't cheat,' Ernie said matter-of-factly. 'Ask me something now. Something really difficult. I bet you I can answer it.'

Before I could think of anything sensibly hard to ask, Lenny blurted out, 'Do almonds have nipples?'

'What?' Ernie and I both blurted back.

'Answer the question, wise guy,' Lenny said.

Ernie frowned, shook his head, then said, 'No, Lenny, almonds do not have nipples.'

'Ha! Wrong!' Lenny said triumphantly. 'They *do* have nipples and there's a carton of almond milk in my fridge that proves it! So tell us, Ern, how did you cheat? Are you wearing a wire? Is someone feeding you the answers through an earpiece?'

'Almonds don't have nipples, Lenny,' I said out of the side of my mouth.

'Where does the milk come from then? Now shush, Agatha. I have him cornered and I think he might be about to spill.'

'She's right, I'm afraid,' Ernie said. 'Almonds do not have nipples. But they are a good source of magnesium, molybdenum, riboflavin and phosphorus, as well as vitamin E, manganese, biotin and copper.'

'I do not understand these words you speak. Magnee-see-yum, phos-for-us, manga-geese?' Lenny slapped his hand over his mouth. 'Agatha! I told you!'

'Told me what?'

Lenny put his hand on Ernie's shoulder. 'You're speaking Alienese, aren't you?' Then he lowered his voice to a whisper. 'Blink if the aliens have got you. We can help.'

Ernie stared at Lenny, not blinking.

Lenny waited.

Ernie stared at Lenny, not blinking.

'It's not aliens,' I said, after more time than I should have allowed. 'It's never aliens, Lenny. Come on, Ernie, tell us what's going on.'

Lenny put his face closer to Ernie's. 'Just a second more, Agatha.'

And then, because his eyes were beginning to stream, Ernie blinked.

'Aha! I told you!' Lenny said.

'The aliens haven't got me! That's preposterous!' Ernie said. 'Look, it really was down to training.'

I still wasn't buying it, but then he said something that caused my spy-detective instincts to spark and crackle.

'It was special Minerva training for the Exceptionally Able.'

I didn't need to hear any more.

'I want in,' I said. 'I'm exceptionally able!'

Ernie looked me up and down, like he was

considering it. 'Ms Stranglebum is very keen to see how I do first, but she does intend to invite more children into the scheme eventually. I'll see what I can do.'

Mr Whip appeared at the end of the corridor. 'Ernest Strewdel to the gymnasium, on the double!'

Ernie saluted, then jogged off down the corridor.

I grabbed Lenny by the elbow. 'Let's follow them. I need to see this training for myself!'

Lenny and I crouched outside the double doors to the school gym – a huge, dusty room with a wooden climbing frame attached to the wall.

'Crouch down so I can stand on your back and see through the windows,' I told Lenny.

'I am a person, Agatha, not a step!'

'Lenny, are you a spy-detective or not?'

'I am.'

'Then act like one and make like a step already!'

Lenny huffed, but got on all fours so I could stand on his back.

'What are they doing?' he asked.

'Jogging on the spot. Now lunging . . . star-jumping . . . I think they're warming up. Crikey, Mr Whip really shouldn't squat in those tiny shorts of his. He'll do himself an injury.'

'Agatha, do you think you could get down now?'

'Shh, they've stopped. They're going to the ropes.'

'Ernie can't climb a rope!'

'He can now!'

I watched, open-mouthed, as Ernie Strewdel, the person who held the school record for the number of notes given to get out of PE, shot up the rope like a ferret up a drainpipe. He then dropped down from the top, landed on the ground and commando-rolled, avoiding the basketball that Mr Whip had launched at him.

'I don't believe my eyes!' I said, because I couldn't.

'Again!' Mr Whip bellowed. 'But faster!'

Ernie scurried up the rope again, this time with Mr Whip hurling basketballs at him as he climbed. Ernie took evasive action, dodging them all, except the last, which he caught one-handed. He then threw the ball across the hall and scored a goal in the basketball net.

'Wow,' I said. 'Ernie's amazing!'

Mr Whip didn't seem impressed, though. 'Stop showboating, Strewdel, and get down and give me a thousand!' he barked.

Ernie leaped to the floor and immediately started bashing out one thousand press-ups.

I could have watched him for ages, but the sound of **'UNAUTHORIZED PUPILS IN CORRIDOR!'** startled me so much I tumbled off my step. I landed with my legs either side of Lenny like I was riding a horse.

The robot-librarian owl squawked another warning. **'LEAVE THE BUILDING IMMEDIATELY! SCHOOL IS CLOSED!'**

'You heard it,' I said, and gave Lenny a little kick to get him going. 'Gallop out of here, partner!'

'Agatha,' Lenny said quite angrily. 'No.'

'Fine.' I jumped off. 'We can run!'

We raced round the corner and headed for the door, the owl chasing us the whole way. When we got outside and were far enough from school, I said, 'You should have seen it, Lenny! Ernie is incredible! If I'm going to stand any chance of beating him, I need to get myself on to that special Minerva training programme for the Exceptionally Able!'

'But, Agatha,' Lenny said, his eyes all goggly, 'what if it's dangerous? I don't trust Minerva at all! Think of the robot-owl librarians and how bad they've become! Look what's happened to Ernie – he isn't Ernie any more! What if it changes you into somebody else?'

'Somebody *better*, though? Come on, you have to admit new Ernie is a vast improvement on the old one!'

'But I *liked* the old Ernie and I like you! I don't want you to change! You're great as you are.'

It was a nice thing to say. But I wasn't really listening, and I guess I didn't really believe what Lenny said about me being great the way I am. I was too busy imagining my name at the top of the leader board. Me walking the halls in a special blazer. Everyone knowing who I was and knowing that I was worth something, even my parents.

'Look,' I said, 'it'll be fine. I need to investigate what's really going on with Minerva, from the inside.'

This was a bit of a lie.

At that moment, I didn't care what was going on with Minerva. I told myself it was a good thing – an environmentally friendly thing, probably – even if, deep down, I had my doubts. But really I just wanted to be in the special training programme. I wanted to stand out. To be the best. Number one. The top. First. Something that I never, ever was at home. Not with my huge family.

Lenny looked at me with a very scrumply-faced expression. 'I just think we should look into it more before you sign yourself up.'

'Trust me! It will be absolutely fine,' I said.

Which was wrong. But maybe if Lenny had believed me he wouldn't have had to turn to Gregor and then managed to do what he did. So really what happened next was a bit my fault, but still mainly his.

CHAPTER 9
LENNY

There's no need to point fingers at who was to blame for what happened next, but, if there was, all my fingers and toes would be aimed fully in the direction of Agatha Topps. I mean, if she had listened to me when I said there was something fishy going on, maybe she would have been there in the basement to tell me what transmogrification *actually* was. Maybe I wouldn't have pressed the button under the big warning sign that said DO NOT PRESS THIS BUTTON.

But she didn't, and she wasn't, and I did, so in my eyes she is entirely to blame.

Even though she said she wanted to do some spy-detectivizing of Minerva 'from the inside', I was beginning to think Agatha wasn't interested in the mission at all. Over the next week, she didn't listen to any of my plans, just spent more and more time on her Pedal-Pod™ – at lunch, at break, even after school – desperately trying to beat Ernie, but failing miserably. She was also getting grumpier and grumpier that she hadn't been invited on to the special training programme for the Exceptionally Able yet.

I couldn't wait for that to happen. I had to get to the bottom of what was going on – with or without her help. But for that I needed a new assistant, and there weren't many candidates for the role. In fact, there was only one person – or gargoyle – who I knew would jump at the chance.

'Och no!' Gregor said when I went to meet him in the attic early one Thursday morning.

I couldn't believe my earholes. 'What do you mean, *och no*?'

'I've decided to keep ma nose oot o' suspicious activities,' Gregor said. 'I'm all aboot keepin' ma'self to ma'self these days. Now, would you scratch ma bahookie with that plank o' wood? Ma Creeping Crevice Moss is itchin' summat rotten.'

'No! Getting someone else to scratch your bum for you is very much not keeping to yourself! And listen, I'm offering you a chance of promotion to my number-one spy-detective assistant!'

'Temptin', but I think I'll pass.' He picked up an old brick and started chomping on it. 'I'll tell ye what: next time ye visit, bring me somethin' wi' a wee bit more flavour, eh? Somethin' exotic, like a nice bit o' patio, or a tasty morsel from a rockery. I'm a wee bit bored o' the bricks up here.'

'You should definitely come to the basement with me then. I hear they have some *delicious* stonework down there,' I said very cleverly.

Gregor's eyes opened wide, but he didn't say anything.

'Real vintage brick apparently,' I continued. 'Mouth-watering masonry. Mmm! So crunchy and crumbly . . .'

'Hmmm, vintage,' Gregor said and licked his lips. 'Och well, when ye put it like that, maybe a wee visit wouldnae hurt . . .'

I didn't care if he did do a wee down there. I had been super cunning and got him to assist me. I didn't need Agatha. In fact, I had a feeling right down in my belly button (just next to the mole I call Bernard) that, at this precise moment, *she* needed *me*.

Gregor agreed to meet me at the end of the day and I went back down to the classroom, excited that I was going to embark on my very own secret mission.

Jordan met me in the doorway.

'Where've you been?' he said.

I remembered the training Agatha had given me in resisting interrogation when you have somthing to hide – stay calm and say nothing.

'Nothing.'

Jordan frowned. 'That doesn't even make sense! What do you mean, *nothing*?'

'Nothing,' I said again.

'What?' Jordan spat. 'I asked you a question!'

'Nothing,' I repeated.

'You've been with that weird grey pet of yours again, haven't you? I know it exists . . . What do you say about that?'

'Hmmm . . . nothing?'

Jordan looked like he was about to self-combust, but I was really quite pleased with how I was handling such intense questioning.

Luckily, before Jordan could actually explode, Miss Happ shouted, 'Boys, come and sit down immediately! I need to tell you about the museum trip next week!'

★

The hours stretched slowly in a long blur of pedalling. After the end-of-school klaxon had sounded, I met Gregor as planned in the boys' toilets. We waited until the school fell silent and the coast was clear. Then, keeping an eye out for the robot owls, we scurried to the school office where Gregor phoned my mum to explain why I was going to be late home.

'Tell her I'm at a sports fixture or something,' I said, handing Gregor the phone.

'Mrs Tuchus, this is Dr Errno callin' to inform ye that yer wee laddie, Lenny, will be late home today because he has been selected fer the sports team.'

I heard Mum squeal with delight, then pause and say, 'What team?'

'The, erm, caber-tossin' team,' Gregor said. 'He's shown great talent fer the sport!'

I put my thumbs up. I reckoned I'd make an excellent caber tosser.

'*Really*?' I heard Mum say. '*My* Lenny?'

'Aye. Unexpected fer sure,' Gregor continued, 'what wi' his puny arms, but there ye go. We'll drop him back once he's finished hurlin' logs.'

Then he hung up before Mum could say anything else.

With that sorted, we crept silently along the corridor towards the stairs down to the basement – or I did anyway.

'Can you creep a bit quieter?' I whispered to Gregor.

'I'm made o' stone!' Gregor said. 'Creepin' is no' really ma area o' expertise.' He lifted one foot and pointed at it. 'These are not exactly built fer sneakin' around. Bahookie-kicking, on the other hand . . .'

'Well, just try!' I said as we turned a corner – right into the path of Jordan Wiener.

I reacted quickly, picked up Gregor and launched him through the open door of Miss Buttercup's classroom. He landed with a bit of a crash.

Jordan said, 'What was that?'

'Nothing?' I said innocently.

'Don't start that again! That wasn't nothing!' Jordan stomped up to me. 'Was that *the thing*? It was, wasn't it!' He poked his head into the classroom, then frowned. 'I'm sure you threw something in here.'

'Nope.' I peered into the classroom too. I couldn't see Gregor anywhere.

Jordan frowned. 'I swear I saw –'

'Nothing,' I said.

He fixed me with a squinty-eyed glare. 'I'll give you nothing!'

'Er, OK. I'm actually fine with you giving me nothing.'

'I didn't mean *nothing*. I meant – Oh . . . oh, bog off, Tuchus!' he yelled. And then bogged off himself down the corridor.

When Jordan was safely out of sight, I hiss-whispered, 'Gregor, where are you?'

'Up here.'

Gregor was wedged between the door frame and the ceiling.

'How did you get up there?'

'I'm a gargoyle,' he said, wiggling his talons at me. 'We're designed to cling on to walls.'

'Nice!' I said. 'Now let's get going, but how about a little less noise this time?'

'How aboot a wee bit less gargoyle-tossin'?'

Anyway, by some miracle, we made it down the stairs to the basement door without alerting Cleaner Wiener, Dr Errno or any of the robot owls to our presence. I tried the handle, but it didn't open. Matzo balls! Where was Agatha and her uncanny ability with doors when I needed them . . .?

Gregor gave the door a hard kick and it swung open.

'Bahookies and doors,' he winked and walked through, sniffing the air for bricks. I followed; no time for nerves.

The basement was vast – as big as Gregor's

room in the attic – and it didn't take a genius to figure out that something odd was going on down here. Something *very* odd.

Rows of computers and monitors lined the walls. There were also a few Pedal-Pods™ and something that looked like a huge battery, with glowing green lights on the side that read **84%**. 'That must be where all the energy from the pedalling ends up,' I said. 'I wonder where it goes from here?'

'Probably powerin' all these whatchamacallits and oojamaflaps,' Gregor said, gesturing around.

Strange equipment filled the room – glass boxes with light crackling through them, huge metal coils thrumming with energy.

'None of this looks like it will save the ice caps, or the rainforests, or the blue-footed booby, does it?' I said.

Gregor shook his head gravely. 'No, unless the blue-footed booby wants its neurons accelerated.' He pointed at a large metal helmet mounted on the wall with Neuron Accelerator™ printed on it in bold lettering.

'What's a neuron?' I said in a trembly voice. 'Is it another word for alien? I'm sure we did something about neuron stars in science once.'

'I have no idea, laddie,' Gregor said. 'But this isnae like any basement I've ever seen. More like some kind o' laboratory. Where's the vintage brick ye promised me?'

'Forget the masonry! Is that a sheep?' I said, pointing at a sheep.

Gregor nodded solemnly. 'I believe it is,' he said.

And then the sheep gave a little meow.

Out from behind a huge machine with MUSCLE MULTIPLIER 2000™ emblazoned across the side, a cat suddenly appeared. I bent down to stroke it, and it baaed happily.

Now maybe Agatha might have seen this as a warning sign – but we did not. Sheep and cats are, after all, very closely related; I think, in the animal kingdom, they are first cousins or something like that.

But my attention was forced away from the sheep-cat and cat-sheep by two huge egg-shaped pods, each a bit bigger than a postbox. Above them was a sign that said TRANSMOGRIFICATION CHAMBERS™.

'Trans . . . mog . . . rif . . . ication,' I said slowly, allowing the word to enter the vortex that is my super-brain. It took only about twenty-three seconds for me to compute the meaning of those eighteen letters, but, as soon as I figured out what they meant, I double-fist-pumped the air and did a little skippety-jump. I had wanted to transmogrify for as long as I could remember.

But that was because I thought *transmogrification* meant *teleportation*. Obviously, I know better now. But I didn't then, and I wanted to try it. Immediately. Because how cool would that be – being warped from one place to another? If it worked, maybe I could transmogrify myself over to MI5 headquarters to see my dad!

Completely forgetting we were in the middle of a mission, I stepped over the baaing cat-sheep and whooped, 'Gregor! Get in there!', bustling him into the first chamber before he could protest. 'It'll be fun!' I said and slammed the door behind him.

I jumped into the other chamber and closed the door.

'Get ready to swap places!' I shouted and rubbed my hands together in excitement.

In front of me were a load of switches and dials

that made no sense. Apart from one: a huge red button that said DO NOT PRESS THIS BUTTON UNLESS . . . *blah-blah-blah* . . .

I knew that was the one for me.

Without a second thought, I thumped the button, and heard the door lock, before a humming shook the chamber.

The air started to fizz and crackle and all the hairs on my body – of which, admittedly, there are not many – began to stand on end. Then came a whoosh, and a blinding light, and a feeling like my brain was being turned inside out.

The light faded and there was a slight smell of smoke, as if somebody had burned bacon. I also had a weird feeling that the chamber had got bigger somehow. I opened the door, stepped out and heard the door next to me open too.

But, instead of Gregor, it was me who stepped out of the other chamber. *Another* me. A perfect copy of me. I was understandably a bit confused, so I said, 'Lenny . . .? Wait . . .What?! *I'm* Lenny.'

Other me frowned then said, 'Och, Lenny, ye wee bampot! It's me, Gregor! But why do ye look like a gargoyle?'

'Like a what?' I said very slowly.

'Ye look exactly like me! A dashingly good-lookin' gargoyle! A vast improvement, I'd say!'

A cold feeling swept through my body.

No, I thought. *It can't be.*

I rushed over to one of the shiny metal machines to check out my reflection. But staring back at me was a gargoyle.

I had turned into Gregor.

The machine hadn't swapped *where* we were – it had swapped *who* we were! I was inside Gregor's body and he was inside mine.

I screamed.

Gregor came up beside me and saw what I was screaming about.

He turned to me and screamed.

I screamed again.

Then he screamed.

And then we both screamed together at the same time.

After we'd finished screaming, we screamed

a little bit more.

Eventually, Gregor said, 'Can we stop screamin' now?'

'*What else can we do?*' I screamed.

'Maybe we can use the machine to swap back?'

I stopped screaming. That was actually quite a good idea. *Agatha had better watch out*, I thought. She could lose her assistant role for good if Gregor kept this sharp thinking up.

We jumped back into our chambers and I pressed the button again. The chamber hummed for a moment, but then the humming died down without any flashes or whooshes. It wasn't working.

I looked over to the big battery. It was now flashing red and said **0% – *INSUFFICIENT POWER***.

Matzo balls! We had used all the energy on the first transmogrification, and now there wasn't enough to swap us back!

So Gregor and I decided to go back to our original plan – screaming – until my throat ached. Our mission to discover what Minerva was up to had not gone brilliantly.

Much as it pained me to admit it, we needed the help of a proper assistant.

We needed Agatha Topps.

CHAPTER 10
AGATHA

Very annoyingly, even though Ernie had told me he would speak to Ms Stranglebum about getting me on to the Minerva training programme for the Exceptionally Able, he spent the next week coming up with excuses why it wasn't happening. I think he didn't want the competition.

First, he'd said that it would happen after some important challenge he had to complete, and that my progress was being monitored apparently. When the time was right and Ms Stranglebum was satisfied with my commitment, they would bring me in.

Well, if they wanted commitment, I'd show them commitment. Thinking about a special blazer and my very own underling and making my parents proud, every lesson I pedalled like I had never pedalled before. Each day Ernie came top of the school leader board, but I was never outside the top three, just behind him and some kid in Year Six. My points were racking up. Surely I'd get the call soon. I just had to keep focus.

Which wasn't always easy because Lenny kept badgering me about investigating Minerva. He was worried for me, he said. But I wasn't interested in investigating – seriously, how could saving the planet be a bad thing? And frankly I didn't have time. I was undertaking my own training programme until Minerva enrolled me in theirs.

This basically involved eating nothing but pasta and boiled eggs, and taking ice baths every night. It's what all elite athletes do.

It was after ice bath number six, when I was lying in bed, trying to get warm again, that I heard a scrabbling noise, followed by a knocking on my bedroom window. 'Agatha, it's me! Let me in!'

Luckily, my two brothers Tom and George,

who usually slept in the top bunk, had moved into the babies' room, blaming my egg-based diet on why they could no longer share with me. I climbed out of my bottom bunk and went to see why Lenny was here.

I pulled back the curtains, but it wasn't Lenny who was clinging to my window frame – it was Gregor, with his nose pushed up against the glass.

I opened the window and he fell face-first on to the floor with a sound like a dropped boulder.

'Shh, what are you doing here, you naughty gargoyle?' I said.

'Agatha, we've got a problem!' Gregor whimpered.

'Where's Lenny?' I knew instantly that any problem *had* to involve him.

As if on cue, Lenny fell into my room, licking what looked like one of the ornamental squirrels from our neighbour's garden.

I grabbed it out of his hands. 'Lenny! Why were you licking this squirrel?'

Lenny didn't answer. Instead, he pulled a gnome out from under his jumper, said, 'Curse these fragile teeth,' and started licking that.

Confused, I turned to Gregor. 'Is that the problem? Lenny's started to lick garden ornaments?'

Gregor grabbed hold of my arms and looked at me with huge, desperate, goggly-boggly eyes.

'That's not Lenny, Agatha! *I'm* Lenny.'

I said, 'You what now?' Because clearly I know the difference between my best friend and a Scottish gargoyle.

'Och, it's true, lassie,' Lenny said, sadly licking the gnome and sounding very much more Scottish than usual.

'Stop that!' I said, snatching the gnome off him. 'What exactly is going on? Why are you here, slobbering over garden ornaments and sounding Scottish in the middle of the night? Explain yourself this instant, Lennox Tuchus!'

'We did some spy-detectoring,' Gregor said.

'And, because you didn't want to come, I took Gregor as my assistant instead and we made a bit of an . . . oopsie.'

'Why are you talking about yourself in the first person, Gregor? And what do you mean – *we did some spy-detectoring*?'

I did not like the sound of unofficial spy-detectoring going on without me. I was slowly getting a feeling that Lenny had done something very, very wrong. Way wronger than squirrel-licking.

'The cat-sheep was probably a clue, but I thought they were just cousins,' Gregor continued sadly. 'I don't think Minerva is doing anything very environmentally friendly.'

'Cat-sheep?' I stammered. 'I . . . I . . . what?'

'I think one of them must have pressed the red button too. I reckon it was the sheep. They always look untrustworthy to me.'

'Gregor, what are you talking about? What sheep?' I spluttered.

'Agatha, do you know what *transmogrification* means?' Gregor's voice was very shaky, but still not very Scottish. 'Because I thought I did. But it turns out I didn't.'

'Transmogrification?' I looked from Gregor to Lenny, then back to Gregor again. 'Why are you talking about transmogrification?'

I said that very slowly, not wanting to hear the answer, which I had a strong suspicion was coming.

Gregor gave me an apologetic smile. 'Because we accidentally did a spot of transmogrificationing, and I am now inside the body of Gregor and he is now inside the body of me.'

'*Yaaaaaawhaaaaaaa . . .?*'

I paused. Those weren't words. I tried again.

'*Naaaaaaah . . . ohhhh . . . naaaaaah?*'

I blinked and looked at Gregor and Lenny, who both nodded at me sorrowfully.

'*Sheeeeeeeeeeessssssssssssshyyyyyy MAMMA!*'

I sank down on to the carpet. And didn't say anything for quite some time.

'Agatha?' Gregor said eventually. Well, it was actually Lenny who was in Gregor's body, but I was still processing that new information. 'Did you get what I said?'

'You accidentally did a spot of transmogrification? Who even does that? I mean . . . WHAT? WHERE? WHEN? WHAT? WHY?'

'I shall answer your queries in a methodical spy-detective manner,' Lenny-in-Gregor's-body said, and held out a knobbly finger. 'Who does that? Well, me and Gregor does that.'

He held out another finger. 'What? I know! We were surprised too.'

A third finger. 'Where? In the Minerva lab, in the school basement.'

A fourth finger. 'When? During our investigation

that you refused to come on yet still somehow managed to mess up.'

He then went to hold out another finger and realized there wasn't one there. He looked at Gregor-in-Lenny's-body. 'You only have four fingers?'

Gregor held up his own hands. 'No' any more! I have five! *Ewwww!* Five!'

Lenny gulped and carried on, quite bravely actually, considering his finger discovery.

'And why? Well, there was this big red button – you know the type – and it just had to be pushed! Ask the cat-sheep. She knows what I mean!'

All this information sort of bounced around in the bit between my skull and my brain, trying to get in. It took a while because I really did NOT want to believe what they were telling me was true. But then I looked at Gregor, who was staring at me with big, bulging, terrified eyes, and at Lenny, who was gnawing on my bedpost, and there was absolutely no way of avoiding the truth.

Lenny had gone out spy-detectoring without me and had a disaster. I suppose I always knew this would happen one day. But I didn't expect him to do something quite so spectacularly catastrophic.

'You've swapped bodies,' I said flatly. 'The two of you went out ONE time and you've managed to swap bodies?'

Lenny nodded his knobbly gargoyle-y head. 'Uh-huh.'

'Lenny, this is quite something, even for you.'

But, as much as I was shocked, alarmed, appalled, surprised and yet somehow not *that* surprised by what Lenny had managed to do, I also knew we now had a proper mystery to work on. While what Lenny had done was one billion per cent a catastrophic disaster of the most gargantuan kind, he had also uncovered some very interesting new information.

There was a secret Minerva laboratory in Little Strangehaven Primary! With Transmogrification

Chambers™! And what on earth could Transmogrification Chambers™ have to do with saving the environment? Minerva Industries were up to something else. Something top secret and probably very bad, if the robot librarians were anything to go by. And I had to get to the bottom of it.

'What else did you find in this secret laboratory?' I asked. 'Tell me everything!'

'All sorts!' Lenny-in-Gregor's-body said. 'A giant battery where all the Pedal-Power energy gets stored. Loads of computers. Something to do with aliens –'

'It's never aliens, Lenny,' I reminded him.

'Well, there was a Neuron Accelerator helmet™! That's gotta be to do with neuron stars, which means space, which means aliens!'

'Lenny, neurons are inside your head!'

'They're not – they really exist!'

'No, I mean that neurons are literally part of your brain – they're what make it work! If it works, a Neuron Accelerator™ would make you cleverer. And I'm thinking that's how Ernie's got so smart! You had to try the body-swapping machine and not the brain enhancer, didn't you?'

I paused and took a breath. 'Clearly, Minerva must have all that stuff in there for a reason. We'll have to go in again, get you two swapped back and find out what the heck is going on.'

CHAPTER 11

LENNY-IN-GREGOR'S-BODY

'**Y**es, I know,' I said. 'It's a real mess. But we need to just move on – it's no good blaming people for being a bad assistant, or pointing fingers at anybody.'

'Lenny, why are you pointing a finger at me?' Agatha asked.

I quickly put my bony grey finger down.

'Right, anyway,' I said, 'the way I see it is that we have two urgent problems to deal with –'

'Only two?' Agatha interrupted.

'The first,' I said, ignoring Agatha, 'is that I have an incredibly itchy bum crack.'

'Och aye, that'll be the Crevice Moss,' said

Gregor-in-my-body, nodding. 'I'm a martyr to it.' He stuck a hand down the back of his trousers. 'I see yer own crevice is blessedly free o' moss. It's as smooth as marble down here.'

'Get your hand away from my bottom!' I shouted at Gregor, who quickly pulled his hand out of his trousers – *my* trousers.

I scratched my bum crack. It was crazy itchy. 'Agatha, do you have any Crevice-Moss cream?'

'Surprisingly, I don't,' Agatha said.

'Matzo balls!'

'Lenny, in the grand scheme of things, your itchy bum is not our biggest concern.'

I ignored her startling lack of consideration and pressed on.

'The second problem is the big one, and that's my mum.' I pointed at my grey, gargoyle-y body. 'If she sees that I've turned into a gargoyle, she'll . . . she'll . . . well, I'm not sure what she'll do, but I don't think she'll be very happy. She might even freak out a bit. She's very fond of my face.'

'Och, I dinnae know aboot that, laddie. She might think it's an improvement,' Gregor said.

'Improbable,' said Agatha. 'It's more likely that finding her only son has turned into a gargoyle might indeed make her freak out. A *lot*. And, while we also have the issues of the weird lab in the school basement and figuring out what Minerva is up to, you're right. You being a gargoyle is our most pressing concern at present.'

'What are we going to do?' I groaned. 'She's expecting me home in an hour!'

Agatha thought for a moment. 'We can't go back to the laboratory tonight, so there's only one thing for it. Gregor is going to have to act like you.'

'But . . . but . . . he's got a Scottish accent!'

'Och, do I? Only a wee hint surely?'

I couldn't believe my grey, pointy ears. 'WHAT? You have such a strong accent you sound like the Loch Ness Monster! AND BEFORE YOU SAY ANYTHING, I KNOW THE LOCH NESS MONSTER DOESN'T TALK.'

'We have no choice, Lenny,' Agatha said gently. 'It's just until we work out how to change you back.'

I fell to the floor. She was right.

'OK, fine,' I groaned. 'Gregor can pretend to be me.'

We spent the next half an hour training Gregor in how to impersonate me. It wasn't easy. After we'd managed to stop him licking his garden gnome, we focused on his accent.

'Helloooooo,' he said in a high-pitched voice. 'Ma naaame is Lenny Tooooshus.'

'That's not how I talk,' I said, rather offended.

'I'm afraid to say it is, laddie!'

'You sound like the Queen! I do not sound like the Queen.'

'That's a matter o' opinion.'

On and on it went until finally we ran out of time – I had to get home.

'OK, hop in,' Agatha said, pointing to my school bag.

'No way!'

'How else are you supposed to get into your house? You can't just waltz through the front door with Gregor!'

I had no intention of waltzing anywhere – gargoyle bodies were not meant for any type of ballroom dancing – but she had a point. It *was* the best way of getting inside the house without being noticed.

So I reluctantly clambered into my own school bag, and Agatha zipped it up. It smelled of bananas and sweaty PE kit in there, but as I like bananas, and it was my own rather lovely-smelling sweat, I didn't mind.

'Goodbye and good luck. I'll start thinking about a plan to get you swapped back and blow the lid on whatever Ms Stranglebum is really doing in the lab,' Agatha said, and before I knew it I felt myself being picked up and slung on to the back of Gregor-in-my-body and we left Agatha's house.

Ten minutes later, I heard the ring of my bell

and then the sound of my mum coming to the door.

'Don't mess this up!' I whispered to Gregor-in-my-body.

My mum opened the door. 'Hello, love – nice day? How was the caber tossing?'

'Oooh, *helllooooo*, Mrs Tuchus – I mean *Mother*!' Gregor-in-my-body said. 'I tossed those cabers like they've no' been tossed before!'

I groaned silently. This was never going to work. But Mum didn't seem to notice.

'Wonderful, darling. I'm so pleased you've found a talent! Finally! Now do you fancy spaghetti on toast for your tea?'

'Oooh, that sounds positively *deliiiiightful*,' Gregor said.

'You're being very polite today!' Mum said. 'It's lovely that you're finally showing some good manners!'

How dare she? I fumed. I *always* had good manners. I never forget to say 'excuse me' after I fart at the dinner table.

A few minutes later, Gregor-in-my-body was sitting at the kitchen table, a plate of steaming spaghetti in front of him. I was still squashed in the school bag at his feet, the smell of food making my round, grey stomach rumble.

'Don't sit there staring at it! Eat up!' Mum said.

A few moments later, Gregor-in-my-body said, 'Thish food ish very soft and pulpy. Would ye have any gravel to scatter over it?'

I winced.

'Any . . . gravel?' Mum repeated uncertainly.

'Aye! Or even a few small pebbles? To add a wee crunch.'

'Pebbles . . .? Lenny . . . are you feeling OK?'

'Och aye – I mean yes! I . . . er . . . am feelin' absolutely tip-top!'

'But you're talking about eating gravel, darling,' Mum said, her voice full of concern. '*And* you keep slipping into a Scottish accent.'

That's it – we were rumbled. Done for.

'Aye,' said Gregor-in-my-body. 'I . . . er . . .

might have overexerted ma'self at the caber tossin'. I'm feelin' a wee bit oot o' sorts.'

I heard my mum gasp. 'Well, you need to rest! Upstairs with you! Bed immediately, my poorly poppet.'

Fortunately, Gregor-in-my-body knew to keep his trap shut and not say another word. He grabbed the bag with me in it, and, five minutes later, Mum had tucked him up in bed. I heard her give him a squelchy kiss on the forehead.

'Now you just rest, darling, and call me if you need anything. Goodnight, Lenny-loo-loo.'

'Goodnight, Mrs . . . Mum,' Gregor-in-my-body said.

Once the door closed, I jumped out of the bag and stretched my legs. Somehow we had got away with it! Which was brilliant, but also a little concerning that my own mother didn't realize Gregor-in-my-body wasn't her actual son.

I was surprised, though, to see Gregor had tears in his eyes.

'What's up?' I asked.

'She kissed me!' He choked with emotion.

'What?'

'Your mother. Kissed me. Right here,' he said, pointing at his forehead. 'I've never been kissed before.' He looked at me, eyes glistening. 'She's . . . so beautiful.'

'WHAT?'

'Fierce, like a warrior-maiden, but heavenly, like the moon reflectin' on a still loch at midnight.'

'WHAT?' I repeated because I had literally no idea what else to say.

'Lennox Tuchus, I think I might have fallen in love wi' yer mammy.'

CHAPTER 12
AGATHA

After Gregor-in-Lenny's-body and Lenny-in-Gregor's-body left my house, I would like to say that I immediately sprang into action to figure out what on earth we were going to do next. But, in reality, I curled up in a ball on my carpet and rocked back and forth for a while.

The terrible thought that Lenny might be permanently stuck in Gregor's body kept bouncing around in my brain. I wanted him back, in his own body again, being my slightly ridiculous assistant and very wonderful friend. I wouldn't be able to see him half as much if he was stuck up on the school roof, trying to make it as a gargoyle.

Overwhelmed by all the big feelings I was having, I did a full-body sob and said out loud,

'He won't ever learn to ride a bike now. Not with those tiny grey legs – his feet will never reach the pedals. Why oh why didn't I teach him when I had the chance?'

After a few moments of crying, I pulled myself together and realized something. None of this was my fault! Why was I blaming myself?

'Agatha,' I said out loud again, 'you must sort out this mess that Lenny Tuchus has caused. If he never rides a bike because he's turned himself into a gargoyle, that's on him. But he is your friend and you've got to at least try. The daft doofus needs you. So get thinking!'

I really am very excellent at pep talks – completely motivational, in fact, because, in that same instant, I had a plan. Well done me. I wiped my nose on my sleeve, jumped to my feet and began pacing the room.

Yes, my plan could work . . . It was brilliant in its simplicity. I just needed to get into the school basement to look at those Transmogrification

Chambers™ myself. If *Lenny* had been able to use them to swap bodies with Gregor, I was certain I would be able to figure out how to get more energy and swap them back.

And, once the small matter of getting the correct dunderhead back into the correct dunderhead's body was done, I would spend some time spy-detectivizing about the place. I needed to know why Minerva had a secret science lab with body-changing machines and Neuron Accelerator helmets™ in it in the first place.

My spy-detective senses started tingling big time. Something was happening at Little Strangehaven. I could see it so clearly now. I'd been blinded by the chance of getting to the top of the leader board and my own special blazer and my own Lenny – I mean *underling* (why do I keep doing that?) – but now I'd seen the light.

A school with an army of robot librarians.

A school with a secret lab powered by continually pedalling students.

A school where Ernie Strewdel suddenly becomes the fittest, smartest kid overnight.

That was all as weird as a sheep-cat.

And it centred around Minerva and Pamela Stranglebum. She was up to something and I had a boy in a gargoyle's body that suggested that it wasn't something environmentally friendly. Whatever it was, I was the spy-detective to stop it.

That night, despite the utter shambles Lenny had managed to create, I went to bed feeling fired up about having a new case and much more positive about being able to get Lenny and Gregor swapped back.

I sent Lenny a message to let him know the plan for the next day and whispered a silent prayer that they had managed to fool Mrs Tuchus into believing everything was completely normal. Then I closed my eyes, ready to do some seriously excellent spy-detective work the following morning.

★

The next day was Friday, and I had arranged to meet Gregor-in-Lenny's-body and Lenny-in-Gregor's-body *really* early outside school so we could start my investigation before anyone arrived. I told my parents that I was going in for a breakfast science club, which wasn't that much of a lie considering that I was intending on experimenting with the Transmogrification Chambers™ and my best friend and best gargoyle.

As I approached the school gates, I could see someone ahead of me. I could tell by the shape of his bicycle helmet that it was Ernie. He was probably off for more Minerva training. That was something I'd have to get to the bottom of too. Maybe Ernie was training for more than just pedal points . . .

Gregor-in-Lenny's-body stood by the main doors. He had a flower in his hand and was pulling off the petals one by one.

'She loves me, she loves me not. She loves me . . .'

'Who is he talking about?' I asked.

'Nobody,' Lenny-in-Gregor's-body said quite stroppily from under the bush where he was hiding. Then, before Gregor could pull off any more petals, Lenny grabbed the flower and stuck it into his gargoyle mouth and swallowed it with a great big gulp. 'She loves you not,' he said very definitely.

I was very confused. 'Lenny, you just ate that flower. Why?'

'Don't want to talk about it.'

Gregor-in-Lenny's-body took hold of my hands, looked at me with his dark brown eyes and said, 'I'm in love, Agatha!'

'You're in love? Who with?' I asked.

He just gave a big sigh.

'With my mum,' Lenny-in-Gregor's-body groaned, then looked at the ground and shook his big stone head.

'Your mum?' I said. 'But she's old!'

'Not compared to me she isnae,' Gregor-in-Lenny's-body said. 'I've been around fer centuries and never met a woman like her.'

CHAPTER 13

LENNY-IN-GREGOR'S-BODY

Given time, anybody can get used to the greatest hardships. And, like a prisoner who learns to be comfortable in the toughest of jails, I have to admit I was getting quite used to being zipped into my school bag and lugged around by Gregor-in-my-body. It was dark in there, but it was cosy. I almost found myself drifting off as we sneaked towards the basement. That was until I heard a blaring alarm.

'WARNING! WARNING! YOU ARE NOT AUTHORIZED TO BE IN THE SCHOOL BUILDING! RETURN TO THE PLAYGROUND IMMEDIATELY!'

I couldn't see it, but I knew what it was – a Minerva owl patrolling the corridor.

'W-w-we were just –' I heard Agatha stammer.

'BE SILENT! RETURN TO THE PLAYGROUND THIS INSTANT!'

'*You'd* best be silent or I'll bop ye on yer wee glowin' noggin!' I heard Gregor-in-my-body shout.

'YOU HAVE LOST TWENTY POINTS FOR INSOLENCE, LENNOX TUCHUS.'

I groaned inside the bag.

'RETURN TO THE PLAYGROUND NOW!'

'Flap off, ye horrible wee beastie,' Gregor said. 'Can ye no' see we're in the middle o' somethin'!'

'It doesn't look happy,' Agatha said. 'Maybe we should go?'

'Do ye think this proud son o' Scotland is bothered by wha' a mechanical tweety-bird thinks o' him?' Gregor said.

I heard a loud ZAP, followed by a shout of, '*OCHCEEEWOOOWAHHH!* Ma poor bahookie!'

'What's happening?' I squealed.

'The owl just lasered Gregor-in-your-body!' Agatha yelped. 'That's new! Their eyes never zapped before! They're getting worse!'

'Am I hurt? I mean, is ma body hurt? It's no' ma handsome face, is it?'

'Nope, not your handsome face,' Agatha said. 'I mean your regular face.'

'RETURN TO THE PLAYGROUND IMMEDIATELY OR FACE FURTHER PUNISHMENT!'

'I'll give ye further punishment!'

The next thing I knew I was off Gregor-in-my-body's back and being whirled about his head. Round and round in circles I went, wailing, '*WA-WA-WAAAAHHH!*' My stomach bounced from my knees to my eyebrows.

Agatha shouted, 'Go on, get it!'

There was a huge clanging noise of stone on

metal as I walloped into something I guessed was the robot owl. Then the sound of stone on wood as I landed on the ground.

'Well done, Gregor!' Agatha shouted as I struggled out of the bag.

When I was finally free, I staggered about for a moment because I was VERY dizzy and then did a little bit of sick, right on top of the battered robot owl, which was crackling and sparking down one wing.

'*Ewww*,' Agatha said as she kicked the robot owl out of sight under a bush. 'That looks like . . . vomit-concrete.'

'Wha' did ye expect from someone who eats rock?' Gregor-in-my-body said.

'Never really thought about it. Let's get going before –' Agatha stopped short and gasped. 'Quick, hide! Mr Whip!'

Agatha and Gregor ran through the closest door and I ran round in circles and said, 'I feel very dizzy-whizzy.'

Agatha popped back out and dragged me in, closing the door, behind us.

'Where are we?' I said, trying to focus my wibbly-wobbly vision.

'We're in the staffroom,' Agatha said.

'I do not think this is a good place to hide!' I squeaked.

'It's fine – there's no way any teachers will be at school yet. You know they only roll up for the start of lessons,' Agatha said, and turned round to check. 'Wow, would you look at this place! A posh Minerva posh coffee machine. Minerva foot spas. Is that a *hot tub* in the corner? Looks like Ms Stranglebum knows how to bribe her way into a school.'

'What about Mr – Oh cool! A snooker table! And look,' I said, 'a Minerva VR headset and games console!'

'Lenny, we're in the middle of a mission! Remember what happened last time you got distracted?'

'Nope.'

'*Seriously?* You swapped bodies with Gregor!'

Don't know how I forgot about that, to be honest.

'Let's focus on the mission. I reckon Mr Whip must've gone. I'll check if the coast is clear,' Agatha said and put her ear to the door. 'What's that whirring noise?' she said, turning round. 'Gregor! Get off that massage chair this instant!'

Gregor-in-my-body scowled. 'I was enjoyin' havin' ma soft, squashy body mushed aboot.'

'I don't have a soft, squashy body!' I objected.

'No' any more ye don't,' Gregor replied. 'I've got it.'

'Shh!' Agatha snapped snappily. 'What's that noise?'

'It's the massage chair, Agatha,' I said kindly. 'We already figured that out, remember?'

Poor Agatha – sometimes it takes her a while to pick things up.

'No, that other noise!' She pressed her ear back to the door. 'It's Mr Whip again, and he's heading this way! Quick, under the caviar buffet counter!'

We were just about hidden when the door opened. From my position, I could see two pairs of legs. I reckoned they belonged to Mr Whip and Ms Stranglebum because one pair was trouserless while the other was wearing smart high heels.

'Mrs Applebottom has left the massage chair on again,' Mr Whip growled.

'Well, I wish she wouldn't,' Ms Stranglebum replied. 'She'll use up all the energy I require for my laboratory. And I do wish those little twerps could cycle a bit faster. When my enterprise really kicks off, I'm going to need more power. Much more.'

Agatha, Gregor-in-my-body and I all gave each other very spy-detectivey looks.

'I don't want to go back to coal and oil again,' Ms Stranglebum continued. 'I got that whopping great fine last time and had to close the factory because someone was whining about all the emissions.'

Ha! That must have been the fine I found out about when I did my very excellent research!

'I'll go round the classes this afternoon,' Mr Whip said. 'Get the little worms to put their backs into it some more.'

'Good. Now is the product prepared? My clients are important people. You know that – you met most of them in your previous line of work.'

'The product is prepared – in pristine physical shape from the special intensive training.'

'Excellent! I'm off for a mani-pedi. Make sure he's in position for when I return.'

After the door had closed, we scrambled out from under the buffet counter.

'Wowsers,' Agatha said. She had that frenzied look in her eye that she gets when she's really pumped. 'Boy oh boy! Ms Stranglebum really is up to something, and Mr Whip is involved, and it really doesn't sound like she's using the Pedal-Power energy for anything good. We have to get down to that basement! Now! But first does anyone know how long it takes to get your toenails and fingernails done?'

'About an hour,' I said. 'Unless I've left it a while and then maybe an hour and a half.'

Agatha blinked twice, probably impressed by my excellent knowledge. 'OK, Ms Stranglebum looks like someone who keeps on top of her personal grooming,' she mused. 'So let's say we have an hour to do a proper good bit of spy-detective work before she gets back. Synchronize watches!'

'I don't have a watch – I'm a gargoyle,' I said sadly.

'Och, I did have one, but I ate the strap when I got a wee bit peckish,' Gregor-in-my-body said.

'Gregor! My dad gave me that!'

'Forget the watch,' Agatha said unsympathetically. 'We're on a mission!'

'Yes, we are, assistant Agatha. A mission to discover the truth about Minerva! Now follow me!' I said, striding to the door like the excellent leader I am.

'We're not following you anywhere,' Agatha said. 'Back in the bag, brick-for-brains!'

CHAPTER 14

AGATHA

A lot had gone down in the staffroom and my brain was buzzing. With Lenny back in his school bag, Gregor and I hurried along the corridor and down the basement stairs.

I paused outside the door, pressed my ear against it, and listened for voices. There was a soft humming sound, like machines whirring. I took a deep breath and bravely pushed the door open to reveal the most impressive-looking laboratory I had ever seen.

It was the room of all my spy-detective dreams!

'*Wah-wah-woo-wah!*' I said because it completely warranted a *wah-wah-woo-wah*.

Inside, it was exactly like Lenny had said.

There was all manner of impressive-looking machines and equipment, everything branded with the Minerva logo. Among them had to be the Transmogrification Chambers™, which could change Lenny and Gregor back, and the Neuron Accelerator helmet™, which must be behind Ernie's sudden change – we just had to find them. My spy-detective senses also told me that the secret of what Ms Stranglebum was really up to would also be here somewhere. There had to be a reason, a big reason, for all this stuff to be in the basement of Little Strangehaven Primary.

'Look, there's the big battery thing,' Lenny-in-Gregor's-body said, hopping out of his bag and pointing to a big battery thing that read **34%** on the side, in glowing amber letters.

'I think you're right, Lenny. This must be where all the Pedal-Power energy goes. I looked at the mass of wires connecting it to various computers and machines. 'I think Ms Stranglebum is using us kids to power this laboratory.'

I followed one of the wires over to a bench with all sorts of charging ports on it. Attached to them was a range of suspicious-looking equipment: the Muscle Multiplier 2000™, a stun gun, a Shrink-Your-Enemy-To-Amoeba-Size spray™, a long tube with WIND-BLASTER™ on the side. Next to that was what looked like a pair of metal swimming trunks with a load more wires running all around the outside of them. I picked them up – they were quite heavy, which probably meant they weren't designed for swimming.

Gregor and Lenny appeared next to me. 'See, told you there was loads of cool stuff,' Lenny-in-Gregor's-body whispered loudly. 'Ooh, what are these?' he said, reaching for the trunks.

I slapped his knobbly hand. 'Do not touch, Lenny!'

He pulled his fingers back, looking offended. 'Why can't I? You are!'

I didn't go into the whole *because I am the leader and you are my assistant thing*. Instead, I said, 'Because last time you touched something you turned yourself into a gargoyle, that's why!'

'Oh yeah,' he said, like he'd actually forgotten. 'I don't think these will turn me into a gargoyle, though,' he continued. 'Look, it says TRUTH TRUNKS™ on the back.'

'Truth Trunks™?' I said. 'What are Truth Trunks™?'

'There's a label,' Gregor-in-Lenny's-body said, taking them from me.

'What does it say?' I asked, trying to take them back off him, but he held on surprisingly tightly.

'DRY-CLEAN ONLY, DO NOT IRON. Oh and COMFORT DESIGN FOR YOUR BOTTOM TO GET TO THE BOTTOM OF THINGS.' He gave them a lick.

'Put them back. They're not food, Gregor!' I said sternly. 'Now would you two come on? We need to find the Transmogrification Chambers™ and get you both swapped back before Stranglebum shows up. Do either of you remember what the machines look like?'

'Two large egg-shaped pods connected by a

big silver tube, a bit like you get out the back of a tumble dryer,' Lenny-in-Gregor's-body said. Then he stuck his knobbly hand in the air triumphantly. 'Follow me.'

I followed as he scuttled off on his little bow legs. But, before we got very far, Gregor-in-Lenny's-body shouted, 'Ooooh, tingly!' then started giggling. 'There's a disco in ma pants!'

I swivelled round. He had to be kidding!

'Get them off at once!' I hissed because Gregor-in-Lenny's-body had, for some unknown reason, decided to put on the Truth Trunks™ in the middle of my mission. The trunks were vibrating and the lights were flashing across them in a rainbow of colours. 'What do you think you're doing?' I demanded.

'I'm tryin' oot the Truth Trunks™,' Gregor-in-Lenny's-body said honestly.

I couldn't believe it! 'Why?'

'No good reason, lassie,' he said, sounding surprisingly truthful again.

'Do they work?' Lenny-in-Gregor's body said.

'I dinnae know! Ask me a question, Lennster! A question ye couldnae possibly know the answer to.'

Before I could order Gregor to take them off, Lenny-in-Gregor's-body said, 'How much does a bunny carrying an artichoke at noon weigh?'

'*What?*' I snapped.

'I dinnae know,' Gregor-in-Lenny's-body said, which was definitely the truth, because who *would* know that?

'Oh,' Lenny said sadly. 'The Truth Trunks™ are broken.'

While I know I should have told Gregor to take them off, a teeny part of me was curious to discover if the Truth Trunks™ actually worked. I mean, how great would a pair of them be in my line of work?

'Gregor, tell me your biggest secret that you would never tell anyone.'

'I'm no' gonna transmogrify back to being a

gargoyle. I dinnae want to and ye'll never make me do it!'

He slapped his hand over his mouth.

'*You what?!*' Lenny blared.

'Shhhhh, Lenny,' I said. Then I turned to Gregor-in-Lenny's-body. '*You what?!*'

He looked like he was trying desperately not to speak, but he blurted out, 'Fer a woman as wondrous as Mrs Tuchus wouldnae look twice at a gargoyle. So I shall live ma life in the repulsive body of Lenny Tuchus so that I can be close to her.'

'That'd better be you lying right now, Gregor!' Lenny said, his bulgy gargoyle eyes bulging even further out of their stone sockets.

'I speak the truth! Yer mammy is wondrous!' Gregor-in-Lenny's-body yelled. Then he started flailing about, trying to pull down the Truth Trunks™. 'Argh! Get 'em off me! Get 'em off me!' he yelled as he fell to the floor and attempted to wiggle himself free.

'I'm not staying as a gargoyle!' Lenny shot

back as Gregor-in-Lenny's-body writhed about on the floor. 'I can't cope with this bum-crack Crevice Moss much longer! Agatha, tell him! I want my own butt back. I'd not considered it much before, but now I don't have it I really miss my bum. It's so soft and smooth and moss-free!'

'It's ma bahookie now!' Gregor-in-Lenny's-body hollered. Then he shouted, 'Blast these infernal Trunks o' Truth!'

Things were descending into chaos. I needed Gregor out of those Truth Trunks™ quickly.

'Hold still,' I said and unclipped the fastening at the side. The Truth Trunks™ dropped to the floor and Gregor-in-Lenny's-body stepped free.

Lenny-in-Gregor's-body and I stood staring at him.

Gregor shrugged his Lenny shoulders and said, 'Clearly, those dinnae work.' Then he clapped his hands together and said, 'I didnae mean what I said just then aboot no' swappin' back. Shall we continue?' And he strolled further into the laboratory, whistling.

Lenny-in-Gregor's-body shook his bouldery head and smiled. 'I was worried there for a minute.'

Then he set off after Gregor and his body to find the Transmogrification Chambers™, or so I thought.

I thought wrong.

Because, by the time I'd put the Truth Trunks™ back where we found them so no one would realize we'd been in the laboratory, Gregor-in-Lenny's-body was pointing what could only be described as a massive bazooka at Lenny-in-Gregor's-body.

I acted on instinct, cartwheeled across the floor and snatched the gun from his hands.

'Don't move another muscle!' I said, turning the bazooka on Gregor-in-Lenny's-body. 'What's going on?!'

Lenny-in-Gregor's-body flapped an instruction pamphlet in my face and began reading.

'Criminal Camouflage™. Instant concealment! Turn dial to select environment. Aim at subject.

Fire! Your criminal recruit is ready to go – safe in the knowledge that they won't be seen committing illegal activities, thanks to Minerva's state-of-the-art camouflaging. Sounds cool, huh?'

Lenny beamed at me. 'Nice cartwheels by the way – your legs were almost straight and everything!'

'Criminal Camouflage™?'

I looked at the dial on the bazooka, which had been set to standard. There was also an underwater option, desert and jungle settings, strangely a supermarket mode, more strangely still a choice of monk or nun, and finally a pot-luck zoo animal.

'What *is* going on in this laboratory? Why do Minerva have all this stuff?'

'I don't know,' Lenny-in-Gregor's-body said, 'but I really, *really* want to be criminally camouflaged. Pot-luck zoo animal me!'

'Absolutely not,' I said. 'We need to get you into the Transmogrification Chambers™.'

I carefully set the bazooka down, not knowing

that Gregor had already released the safety catch, and, through absolutely no fault of my own, shot myself.

It felt like I'd been hit by an angry blanket. Surprising, but not painful.

'Oh, for goodness' sake!' I exclaimed, looking down at my body, which had been instantly covered in a black Lycra all-in-one bodysuit. 'Look what you've done now!'

'At least it was standard setting, lassie,' Gregor-in-Lenny's-body said.

'Cool,' Lenny said. 'Instant criminal.'

It was cool, but I was absolutely not going to admit that in front of Lenny and Gregor. It would only encourage them to mess about with more stuff. And why would Minerva want to make someone look like an instant criminal?

I pulled the bazookered balaclava off my head. 'Can we please just get on with what we're supposed to be doing?'

'Of course!' Gregor said, just as Lenny picked

up a canister that said INSTANT ESCAPE PARACHUTE™ – SHAKE WELL BEFORE USE.

'Lennox Tuchus,' I growled, 'put that down!'

CHAPTER 15

LENNY-IN-GREGOR'S-BODY

A moment later, I was trying to cram the huge parachute back into the tiny canister.

'I TOLD YOU TO PUT IT DOWN!' Agatha snarled, glaring at me.

I mean, I assume she was glaring at me, but I couldn't actually see her because she was underneath the parachute. But she certainly *sounded* glarey.

'Well, maybe if you were a bit quicker with the warning I might not have accidentally pressed the release button!'

Agatha started flapping about wildly. 'When I get out of this, you're in big trouble, Lennox! What is it with you and pushing buttons you shouldn't?'

Fortunately, by the time she had fought her way out from under the canopy, she'd calmed down a little.

'Are you going to keep that bodysuit?' I asked.

This time I saw her glarey face.

'Can we PLEASE just focus?' Agatha said.

'You're too slow YET AGAIN because I already am ACTUALLY focusing!' I said.

I wasn't going to tell her that what I had been focusing on was a pair of boots with rocket jets attached to the soles.

But Agatha spotted what I was looking at anyway.

'Absolutely not!'

'But – flying boots!'

'No! Lenny, just NO! Can we focus on getting you and Gregor into the Transmogrification Chambers™? Stranglebum will be mani-pedicured soon!'

She had a point. Boots wouldn't solve my

gargoyle-body and itchy-bum situation. I stepped up to one of the transmogrification pods.

'Right, last time Gregor started in this one, so hop into the other, Gregor, and we can swap bodies back!'

Gregor *hmmed* and rubbed his chin.

'Ach now, perhaps we shouldnae be too hasty,' Gregor-in-my-body said, edging backwards. 'These machines can be very dangerous.'

'Gregor, I want my body back,' I said, glowering.

'Well . . . well . . . maybe I dinnae want to swap back!'

'Gregor,' I said, pulling myself up to my full height – which was not very much, as a result of me being stuck in a gargoyle's body. 'GET. IN. THE. MACHINE. NOW!'

'Fine!' Gregor gave an unconvincing laugh. 'I was only kiddin'! I want ma own body back anyway. I dinnae like being this tall. Gives me a wee bit o' vertigo. And yer bum is weirdly smooth. Like two great big apples. I prefer a wee bit o' lichen on ma cheeks – not moss, mind you . . .'

'HURRY UP AND GET IN!' I roared, and that worked.

Gregor-in-my-body clambered into the transmogrification pod with a mournful look on my face.

I hopped into the other chamber, slammed the door shut, and hit the red button, my heart beating with excitement. Finally, I would be back in my own body! Finally, I'd be free of this infernal itching!

But, instead of the humming and fizzing and crackling, nothing happened. I checked myself over: grey skin and knobbly knees, four fingers and big round belly. It hadn't worked.

I looked over at the battery, where the glowing red number on the side said **INSUFFICIENT POWER.**

I stepped out of the chamber, crestfallen.

'Oh dear,' I said.

'Lenny!' Agatha shouted as though it was all my

fault. 'You've drained it with all your messing about!'

I felt terrible, but Gregor-in-my-body actually seemed quite pleased and was doing nothing to disguise his smile.

'Gregor!' I said, giving him a glarey look, which was hard to do because he was in my body and therefore very handsome. 'You used the power up with those Truth Trunks™! You did it on purpose!'

'No! I had nae idea that would happen!' he said, still smiling.

Maybe we shouldn't have played with all that cool stuff after all.

'What can we do now, Agatha?' I wailed.

Agatha checked her watch. 'There's not much time. I say we scram. We'll come back at home time and try again after all the kids have spent the day pedalling and recharged the battery.'

'Shouldn't we look around and try to find out what all this stuff is here for?' I said.

'*Now* you want to stick to the plan?' snapped

Agatha. 'You didn't think about sticking to the plan when you filled my face with parachute! And it's not like Ms Stranglebum will have left the evidence just lying around for us to find.'

'Like this laptop that says PROPERTY OF PAMELA STRANGLEBUM?' I asked.

'Well, yes, but you're not going to be able to access it. It will have all sort of anti-hacker security and –'

'I'm in!'

'What?'

'I'm in. The password was Stranglebum1.'

'Well, great. But it's not like there's going to be all sorts of information on it that we can just –'

'Ooooh! There's a file here called **My Evil Masterplan**.'

Agatha threw her arms in the air. 'Oh, for goodness' sake! What is *wrong* with these people?'

We all gathered round the laptop and Agatha moved the cursor ready to double-click on the file.

CHAPTER 16
AGATHA

I felt mixed emotions about Lenny breaking into Ms Stranglebum's laptop. It was good we were doing some proper spy-detective work and closing in on her Evil Masterplan. Except it wasn't *we* – it was Lenny. I suppose I had given him some excellent training since I'd taken him on, but still.

'I hope you're watching and learning,' Lenny-in-Gregor's-body said as he went to open the Evil Masterplan file.

I harrumphed. I didn't mean to, it just came out. 'Get on with it.'

He didn't get on with it quick enough, though, because a calendar reminder pinged up on the computer screen.

🔔 CONFERENCE CALL

WITH TERRIBLE EVIL CRIME BOSSES

TO DEMONSTRATE PRODUCT BEGINS

IN THREE MINUTES!

We all gasped.

There was even more gasping as the sound of high heels clicked across the laboratory floor.

'Stranglebum must have very small pedis!' I squealed. 'She's back already. Quick – hide!'

I slammed shut the laptop, grabbed Lenny by Gregor's knobbly stone elbow, yanked Gregor by Lenny's arm and dragged them both under the closest workbench. I rammed my finger to my lips to tell them both to be quiet.

We looked at each other with frantic eyes, aware that there was a very real possibility we were about to be discovered by a woman who had a document on her laptop confirming that she was definitely evil.

In absolute silence, we listened as she click-clacked her way towards our hiding place.

I considered making a dash for it – maybe if we surprised her we could be out the door and away by the time she realized anything was going on.

I tried to explain this plan to Lenny and Gregor by using a lot of facial expressions, eyebrow movements and the flapping of my hands, but they, not being trained in silent spy-detective communication, looked at me blankly.

Honestly, you cannot get the staff these days.

Suddenly the footsteps came to a stop. 'What in the –?'

I realized that we had not been one hundred per cent discreet in our investigation of the laboratory in that we – and, when I say *we*, I mean the other two – Lenny had let off an enormous parachute and Gregor the camouflage bazooka.

'Not again,' Ms Stranglebum muttered to herself. 'Honestly, these things. They deploy on their own when you don't want them to, but not when you have a criminal trainee plummeting from a helicopter over an active volcano!'

A criminal trainee?

Her high heels started up again. Heading directly towards us again.

A funny sound filled the air and the footsteps stopped once more.

What *was* that? A sort of crunching, grinding noise.

'Hello?' Ms Stranglebum said. She must have heard it too.

My heart ping-ponged about in my chest as thoughts ping-ponged about in my brain. Did Ms Stranglebum know we were here? Why was Lenny such a disaster-magnet on a mission? Who were these **TERRIBLE EVIL CRIME BOSSES**? What was the product? And, *seriously*, what was that weird sound?

I glanced around. The crunchy-grinding had to be coming from somewhere. It took all my self-control and spy-detective professionality not to roar with fury when I saw it was coming from Gregor-in-Lenny's-body!

He was only gnawing on an instant-parachute canister!

I snatched it from his hands and gave him my most angriest death glare. He had the good grace to look shame-faced.

'Sorry,' he whispered. 'I nibble when I'm nervous.'

'You're going to ruin my teeth,' Lenny-in-Gregor's-body hiss-whispered, which was true, but not our biggest problem.

'Hello?' Pamela called out again. 'Is anyone there?'

We all froze absolutely still – just like statues. Which Lenny-in-Gregor's-body was very good at, what with him being a gargoyle and all.

Ms Stranglebum must have been satisfied with the silence because the footsteps started towards us again, getting closer and closer.

They came to a stop on the other side of the

workbench. Luckily, she didn't stay there long. She picked up her laptop and headed off through a door at the other end of the laboratory.

'That was close!' Lenny-in-Gregor's-body said. 'Let's get out of here!'

'The only place we're going is through that door to find out who these **TERRIBLE EVIL CRIME BOSSES** are,' I said. 'It's time to get our spy-detectivizing on. Now follow me and stay down.'

I commando-crawled across the laboratory floor with Gregor and Lenny behind. When we reached the door, I pressed my ear to it and listened.

Silence.

I rose to my feet and very carefully and slowly opened the door and peeked through the gap. There was a corridor with several more doors coming off it. Above one hung a sign that said MINERVA CONFERENCE ROOM.

Bingo.

I crept up to it, then got to my knees so I could

peer through the chink between the window and a roller blind. Lenny and Gregor did the same, although Lenny had to stand because Gregor's body is a bit on the short side.

Ms Stranglebum was sitting with her back to us at the head of a huge white oval table. On the large screen in front of her were six of what could only be **TERRIBLE EVIL CRIME BOSSES**.

Ms Stranglebum clapped her hands together and said, 'Ladies and gentlemen, thank you so

much for joining me today. You have been selected because you are leaders in the field of criminal activity. I am both delighted and excited to present to you our latest initiative in the Fight Towards Crime – the Minerva Criminal Franchise. I'm certain that, once you've seen my presentation, each of you will want to set up your own franchise in a school near you.'

I gulped. Ms Stranglebum wanted to turn schools into criminal bases!

'A school?' interrupted an evil crime boss lady in a pinstripe suit. 'You can't expect to get away with having a crime headquarters in a *school*.'

'Oh, but I can, and I am! I've set one up right here, in Little Strangehaven Primary. I have a laboratory with all the crime equipment you could possibly want: stun guns, Wind-Blasters™, Shrink-Your-Enemy-to-Amoeba-Size Sprays™, Transmogrification Chambers™ –'

'Ooh, I've always wanted to transport myself somewhere!' said an evil crime boss whose face was mainly moustache and eyebrows.

'See,' Lenny whispered. 'Easy mistake to make.'

'It's a body-swap machine, actually,' Ms Stranglebum continued. 'You name it, I've got it. And it can all be yours too if you choose to buy into Minerva.'

'Yes, but why a school?' the evil crime boss with the moustachey-eyebrow face asked.

'That will become clear if you'll just let me get

on with my presentation and stop asking questions!'
Ms Stranglebum shouted. Then she cleared her
throat and smiled. 'Forgive me – I shall continue.
By joining Minerva, you can also become the
owner of a truly outstanding new product. This
newest . . . weapon, shall we say, is the Future of
Anarchy. I am sure you'll be impressed.'

And, with that, she pressed a button on her
computer.

A hatch opened in the middle of the oval table.
I could sense Gregor and Lenny holding their
breath as we waited to see what dreadful thing
would rise up through the hole.

A nuclear bomb maybe? Or a super-blast laser
gun? Or an invisible grenade-dropping drone?

But it was none of those things. It was
something far more unexpected.

The newest weapon in the Fight Towards
Crime turned out to be none other than Ernie
Strewdel.

CHAPTER 17

LENNY-IN-GREGOR'S-BODY

Now let me tell you: if I hadn't just swapped bodies with a gargoyle, seeing Ernie come out of that table standing beside a Pedal-Pod™ would have been the strangest thing I'd experienced all week. But it was still *very* strange. Agatha and I shrugged at each other.

And the **TERRIBLE EVIL CRIME BOSSES** presumably also thought it was strange too because they all started laughing.

Ms Stranglebum held up her hand. 'Quiet! You are looking at the Future Face of Crime! This child not only commits crime, he provides the power to commit crime.'

'I'm sorry, you've lost me,' said another crime boss. 'You're saying that *kid* is some kind of self-sustaining weapon?'

I liked the look of that boss. He was wearing very cool sunglasses and had a monkey sitting on his shoulder.

'Exactly. Using Minerva's patented Pedal-Pods™, a school of two hundred children can produce enough energy to power all the crime equipment you could ever need. And you'll have no snoopy electricity companies demanding to know why you've racked up a huge bill, or goody-goody governments fining you because your carbon emissions are too high.'

'OK, the pedalling thing I get,' the pinstripe boss lady piped up. 'But he just looks like a regular kid. I don't understand how he can be the Future Face of Crime.'

'Well, if you'll allow me to show you a short video, you will see exactly how,' said Ms Stranglebum, hunching over the computer. 'Now how do you *share screen* on this thing . . .?'

She pressed a key.

'We can't see you!' said the pinstripe boss lady. 'I think you've turned your camera off.'

'I know! One minute . . .' Ms Stranglebum fiddled with some more keys. 'Can you see me?'

'We can *see* you now,' shouted the monkey guy, pointing at his ears, 'but we can't hear you – you're on mute!'

'Oh, for goodness' sake!' Ms Stranglebum huffed, punching buttons angrily. 'There!'

'We can see and hear you now,' said the pinstripe boss lady. 'But you've turned into a talking . . . lemon?'

'That's not a lemon! It's green!' said the evil crime boss with the mainly moustache-and-eyebrow face. 'That's an avocado.'

'Oh yes! Ms Stranglebum, you're an avo–'

'I KNOW I'M AN AVOCADO!' roared Ms Stranglebum. 'It's a filter! I can't turn it off, so you'll just have to ignore it!'

A few more desperate key-thumps and she finally managed to share her screen and clicked play.

'This is a video of Ernest Strewdel from just a few days ago. Observe him.'

We all watched as video-Ernie, sitting at the back of a class, began chewing on a shoelace. Aw – I missed *that* Ernie. Video-Ernie gave a furtive look around to make sure nobody was watching, and then started actually *eating* the shoelace. A few seconds later, the shoelace was completely gobbled up, and video-Ernie looked very pleased with himself. I suppose it was an achievement of sorts, but the **TERRIBLE EVIL CRIME BOSSES** did not look that impressed. Even the monkey was shaking its head. Tough crowd.

Then the video cut to Ernie answering questions from last week's general-knowledge quiz.

'What famous event ended in 1945?'

Ernie's hand shot up. 'That would be 1944.'

Next we saw Miss Happ holding up a picture of a hexagon. 'Name this shape,' she said.

Ernie frowned, then said, 'Bob.'

Miss Happ shook her head and moved on. 'What word rhymes with cart and is also something Vincent van Gogh was very good at?'

'Fart.'

I laughed, but Agatha elbowed me to shush me. I think it hurt her more, though, what with my belly being made of stone.

Ms Stranglebum turned off the video.

'Last week, this boy was an idiot,' she announced.

I thought that was a bit harsh after he'd got all those questions right.

'To prove to you the brilliance of these new Minerva's Minor Menaces™,' she continued, 'this same boy will, in two days' time, single-handedly steal the GIANT RUBY OF KATHMANDU!'

Then she threw her head back and did a very impressive evil villain **wah-ha-ha!**

The **TERRIBLE EVIL CRIME BOSSES** all gasped, which was lucky because it hid my gasp, and Agatha's, and Gregor-in-my-body's whisper-shout of, 'I've always wanted to munch a ruby!'

The evil crime boss with the shoulder monkey leaned forward so he filled the screen. 'It's not possible! This imbecile steal the Giant Ruby of Kathmandu? How? That thing is heavily guarded. It is contained within an impenetrable glass case! Many have tried before and failed.'

Ms Stranglebum stopped **wah-ha-ha!**-ing and said, 'Using the patented Minerva Neuron Accelerator™ (which you will each receive when you buy into the Minerva Criminal Franchise), I have increased his brain capacity by over five hundred per cent.'

'I knew it!' Agatha whispered.

'If you manage to pull off this robbery, you'll be the most widely respected criminal mind in the world!' the pinstripe boss lady said.

'Oh, I know, and the most dangerous!' Ms Stranglebum agreed. 'The Giant Ruby can focus laser beams to make them so strong they can slice the moon in half!'

'Slice the moon in half?' I whispered. '*Cool*.'

'Not cool,' Agatha snapped back. 'Imagine the power an evil crime boss would have if they controlled something like that!'

As if Ms Stranglebum was trying to prove Agatha's point, she said, 'Imagine the power I'll have when I control that! I'll be able to blast all satellites from the sky – those that don't belong to Minerva at any rate.' She did a couple of deep excited inhales through her nostrils. 'I will have total control . . . over *everything*!'

She **wah-ha-ha!**-ed again.

'But *nobody* can steal the Giant Ruby,' the moustachey-eyebrow boss said. 'Let alone a child who eats his own shoelaces.'

'Oh, this boy no longer eats shoelaces,' said Ms Stranglebum. 'Ernie, kindly recite the Greek alphabet.' She gave a sly smile. 'Backwards.'

Ernie nodded, then started speaking in a very strange language I could not understand.

'Interesting,' the moustachey-eyebrow boss said. 'What else can he do?'

'Ernie, is 167,777,423 a prime number?' Ms Stranglebum asked.

'No,' replied Ernie. 'It's divisible by eleven.'

'Is that right?' I whispered to Agatha.

'I don't know!' she snapped. 'My brain hasn't been trained to be five hundred per cent bigger, has it?'

Ms Stranglebum continued, asking impossible question after impossible question, and each one Ernie answered perfectly, to the wide-eyed astonishment of the **TERRIBLE EVIL CRIME BOSSES**, until finally she said: 'Ernie, is it possible to steal the Giant Ruby of Kathmandu?'

Ernie grinned widely. 'Oh yes. Most certainly.'

'You see?' said Ms Stranglebum, turning back to the **TERRIBLE EVIL CRIME BOSSES**. 'Not only have I turned this boy into a genius, but also into an elite athlete through our patented Minerva Exercise Regime™. Thanks to the combination of the Muscle Multiplier 2000™ and the strict training programme overseen by Mr Whip, Ernest Strewdel is now in perfect condition. He has the dexterity to scale walls, the agility to evade capture, and the speed and stamina to outrun even the fittest of police officers.'

She looked at Ernie proudly. 'Endlessly intelligent, physically flawless, utterly obedient. In fact, do a little backflip now for us, please, Ernie.'

Ernie leaped into the air, flipped backwards twice and landed perfectly.

'Matzo balls!' I breathed. 'He really is good!'

'But where does this obedience come from?' asked a crime boss wearing a monocle and a top hat. 'Why would a child agree to become a criminal?'

'Ah, a good question. When the Neuron Accelerator™ is combined with the Corruption Contraption™, the subject becomes not only intellectually advanced, but also bad – very bad.'

'The Corruption Contraption™?' the crime boss said.

We hadn't spotted that one in the laboratory!

'One of Minerva's greatest inventions. Successfully employed on governments around the world for quite some time.' Ms Stranglebum turned to Ernie. 'Tell them how you've changed.'

Ernie's eyes glinted darkly. 'My mind was asleep before, but now it's like I've woken up! I want to do big things. Memorable things. BAD things!'

I really did not like new Ernie AT ALL!

Ms Stranglebum's face split into a smile. 'So you see, ladies and gentlemen, to commit the perfect crime, you need the perfect criminal. And that, my dear criminal brothers and sisters, is precisely what Minerva's Minor Menaces™ are. The jewel in the crown of the Minerva Criminal Franchise bundle.'

All the bosses applauded wildly, even the monkey. I must have got caught up in the moment because I only realized I was also applauding when Agatha elbowed me in the belly again.

Finally, the clapping died down and the pinstripe boss lady spoke.

'Truly, Ms Stranglebum, if that child manages

to steal the Giant Ruby of Kathmandu, you'll be the most dangerous criminal on the planet! If he succeeds, you can count me in.'

The other bosses all made noises of agreement.

'But one last question,' the moustachey-eyebrow guy said. 'Do the teachers not notice their students becoming hyper-intelligent and unfeasibly strong?'

Ms Stranglebum laughed. 'Have you been inside a classroom recently?'

The criminals shook their heads.

'They are awful, harrowing places, full of uncontrollable monsters that drive teachers to the very edge of sanity. You think prison is bad? Prison is *nothing* compared to the average primary school. By the end of most days, teachers are struggling to hold back their tears. If you suddenly turn all their pupils into quiet, well-behaved geniuses, what teacher would say no to that? Besides, they'll agree to anything if you stick a hot tub in the staffroom.'

So there we had it. The full plan revealed –

Pamela Stranglebum wasn't only turning Little Strangehaven into a school for criminal masterminds, she also wanted these **TERRIBLE EVIL CRIME BOSSES** to run other schools exactly the same way. And, if that wasn't bad enough, she was going to steal a giant ruby that could shoot lasers strong enough to split the moon in two!

To be honest, it was a teensy bit worse than I was expecting. But we still had to stop her.

Although first we had to get out of the basement without being spotted . . .

Right after I'd found out whether monkeys were only standard issue for **TERRIBLE EVIL CRIME BOSSES,** or if the good guys were allowed them too.

CHAPTER 18

AGATHA

'Look,' I said as we speed-crawled back along the corridor towards the main laboratory, 'if I agree to consider it, will you focus on the fact that we need to sneak out of here unnoticed?'

Honestly, I couldn't believe we were even having this discussion, but Lenny had decided that, despite currently residing in the body of a stone gargoyle and being within moments of being discovered by Ms Stranglebum, the most urgent issue facing us was whether he was allowed a monkey sidekick.

'Yes, but you have to consider it *properly*, OK? I feel very strongly about this. I don't see why the bad guys should get all the cool pets.'

'Yes, I'll think about it properly,' I said.

However I already had thought about it properly and it had taken me less than half a second to decide that no way was Lenny getting a monkey. The most I was prepared to let him have was a pet snail or a woodlouse or something like that.

'Just imagine! It would be quite the power move on our part. Maybe we should get *bigger* monkeys – really show them we're a match for their evil ways. A gorilla on my shoulder would be *pret-ty* impressive!'

I stopped crawling and gave Lenny-in-Gregor's-body what I hoped he realized was a withering look. 'You want a gorilla to sit on your shoulder?'

He nodded.

'OK, let me know how that works out for you,' I said, and continued to scurry at speed. 'Now can you two pick up the pace a bit? Ms Stranglebum might leave the conference room at any moment and we really have a humongous task ahead of us.'

A klaxon sounded just as we made our way up the basement stairs. I checked my watch.  'Crikey, it's already the end of lunch! We'd better get back to class.'

Lenny-in-Gregor's-body jumped into his school backpack just as a blasted robot-owl librarian appeared. It flashed its laser eyes at us. **'PUPILS IN UNAUTHORIZED AREA!'** it blared out.

'Shurrup, tweety,' Gregor-in-Lenny's-body said, which was brave considering he'd already been lasered in the bum once. Anyway, it was too late. Mr Whip had heard and was storming over to us.

'Where have you been?' he demanded. 'Not in the basement, I hope?'

'No, we're not allowed down there,' I said. 'Why would we go down there? *Is* there something down there, Mr Whip?'

'Absolutely not!' he said, a little flustered.

'Now get out of my sight. I wouldn't want to have to ban you from the museum trip next week, would I?'

'No, sir,' I said. 'I really need to go on that trip!'

He arched an eyebrow. '*Need?*'

'Er . . . yes, for . . . educational purposes, you know. Want to get up that leader board. I have my eye on one of those blazers and a Lenny. Argh! I mean *underling*.'

Mr Whip's eyebrow dropped. 'Then I suggest you both get out of my sight. And Tuchus . . .'

Gregor-in-Lenny's-body did not answer; he was busy staring at the wall as if he was about to try and bite a chunk out of it.

'TUCHUS!' Mr Whip roared.

Gregor-in-Lenny's-body did not answer, so I gave him a nudge.

'Oh aye! That's me!'

Mr Whip shook his head and sighed. 'Just learn to ride a blinking bike, would you?'

And then off he marched towards the staffroom, probably to get a massage.

'Right, we need to discuss what we're going to do next,' I said once he was safely out of earshot. 'No way can we let Ernie steal that Giant Ruby. Ms Stranglebum cannot be allowed to get her wicked hands on something so dangerous. And, if Ernie fails, all those bosses will think that Minerva's Minor Menaces™ are useless and her whole criminal franchise plan will fail too. Let's go back to mine after school and hash out a plan.'

'OK!' came Lenny's muffled voice from inside his school bag.

We hurried off down the corridor and round the corner towards our classroom just as Jordan was going inside.

'Where've you been?' he said. 'You missed all the morning lessons. You're way behind on the points now, *Agatha*.'

I know I shouldn't have cared, what with the fact that the whole points system had been designed to distract me from the school being turned into a hotbed of criminals, but I have to admit that part of me was a little disappointed that I'd lost my lead.

'You've been with that weird grey monster thing with the knobbly legs, haven't you?' continued Jordan. 'I *know* it exists!'

'There is no weird grey monster thing, Jordan,' I replied.

'And if there was,' Gregor-in-Lenny's-body added, 'I think ye'd find it has *exceptional* legs.'

Jordan scrunched up his face into a sneer. 'You're so weird, Tuchus.'

'Well, you're the one who thinks there's a monster running round the school,' I said, and shoved past him.

For the rest of the day, Gregor-in-Lenny's-body did an excellent job on the Pedal-Pod™. He rocketed up the leader board too by answering several difficult questions on history ('Well, I've been around fer hundreds o' years, haven't I?') and geography (he had an expert knowledge on all types of rocks and could spot the difference between igneous and sedimentary from half a mile away).

At the end-of-day klaxon, I grabbed Gregor-in-Lenny's-body by the arm and hurried out of school so we could get to mine quickly to start planning. Halfway there, we hurried back to school again because we'd forgotten Lenny's backpack. Which meant we'd also forgotten Lenny, but that wasn't too much of a problem – he'd fallen asleep so was none the wiser.

I pushed through the gate, jumped over Scooby and Doo (who were chewing a pair of my old trainers), ducked a football (which one of the older twins, Tom and George, had 'accidentally' launched in my direction), shouted a *hello* to Dad (who was in the kitchen feeding the babies, Nigel and Trevor), and a *hello* to Mum (who was combing nits out of Mavis's hair), and slammed the door to my bedroom shut. Then I opened it again, and

hung up a sign to tell Tom and George to keep out.

Gregor-in-Lenny's-body dropped the school bag to the floor and it landed with a bang, which woke Lenny. He crawled out, mumbling, 'Is it the end of lessons already?'

'Yes, and the start of planning our mission to stop Ernie stealing the Giant Ruby and put an end

to Ms Stranglebum and defeat Minerva Industries.
And then we have to work out how to swap you
two back.'

'I actually think swapping me and Gregor back
should be higher priority,' Lenny-in-Gregor's-
body said. 'Like TOP priority, in fact. Not that
you aren't great, Gregor, but I miss my arms and

legs and Bernard the Belly-Button Mole and everything really.'

'Oh, it is absolutely top priority,' I said, nodding.

'It's just that the way you put it last there, in the list of things we need to do, made it seem a bit like it was low priority. Like it was the *least* important thing.'

'No! It's important.'

'VERY important!'

'Yes! We will absolutely focus on swapping you two back. If we have time.'

'NOT *if* we have time! You said we'd go after school, when the battery was recharged from all the pedalling!'

'Sorry, that came out wrong. I didn't mean "if". Of course we'll have time. It's just that I don't think we can risk going back to the laboratory tonight.'

'OK, nae problem wi' me,' Gregor-in-Lenny's-body said very quickly.

'But *whyyyyyyyy?*'

'If we get caught, it could put the whole mission in jeopardy.'

'Oh, Agatha, *pleeeassseee*. You're not the one being lugged about in a bag all day and puking up concrete.'

'I'm very sorry, Lenny, but what if we get captured? We'll be banned from the school trip and then we definitely won't be able to stop Ernie from stealing the Giant Ruby and Ms Stranglebum from getting her hands on the world's most powerful weapon. Then she'll install Minerva Criminal Franchises in schools all over the country! Would you want to be turned evil with the Corruption Contraption™, Lenny? Or be shrunk to the size of an amoeba with that spray?'

'Would you want to be stuck in the body of a gargoyle?' he shot back.

'Nowt wrong wi' the body o' a gargoyle,' Gregor-in-Lenny's-body said.

'Well, *you* don't seem that keen to get back into

it! Why is that, I wonder? It'd better not be anything to do with my mum!'

'No . . . I just happen to agree wi' Agatha,' Gregor said. Then gave a big sigh and added, 'Wha' a woman, though . . .'

'Can we all STOP getting distracted! Lenny, I promise we'll swap you back as soon as we've stopped Ernie getting his hands on that ruby. I want you back too, you know.'

'Fine,' he said and sat down on my bed. 'So how are we going to stop him?'

Before I could tell him the two options I had come up with during the walk home, Lenny raised his little knobbly arm and said, 'Ooh, I know! We could blow up the museum!'

'Er, that would get rid of the ruby, I suppose, but don't you think it's a little bit . . .'

'Much?'

'Yeah, just a little. So what I was actually thinking was –'

Lenny's arm shot in the air again. 'Oooh, I

know! We could commandeer the school bus and drive to Adventureland instead!'

'I think that perhaps people might ask a few questions if we did that. And does anyone here know how to drive? Because I don't.'

Gregor-in-Lenny's-body shook his head, but Lenny shrugged and said, 'How hard can it be?'

'It probably takes a little more skill than riding a bike, and you know how challenging some people find that . . . So, as I was trying to say –'

'*Ooooh*, I know!'

I took a deep breath. 'What now?'

'Nope, sorry, it's gone. I've forgotten.'

'OK. So, as I see it, we have two options. Plan A is to –'

'I've remembered! Let loose a hundred thousand bees into the museum and –'

'NO, LENNY! DO YOU EVEN KNOW WHERE TO GET A HUNDRED THOUSAND BEES?'

'From a hundred thousand hives?'

'There's more than one bee per hive, Lenny! There's more like ten thousand bees in a hive!'

He smiled triumphantly. 'That makes it easier then!'

'OK, well, you go and do that – collect those bees. In the meantime, I will be carrying out Plan A, which is to go to school on Monday, tell Dr Errno everything we know and hope he believes us and reports Ms Stranglebum to the police –'

'Seems a bit boring,' Lenny interrupted.

'So it does,' Gregor said.

I ignored them both. 'And, if that doesn't work, we shall move on to Plan B.'

'What's Plan B?' asked Gregor.

'We unleash my hundred thousand bees!' Lenny said, waving his arms dramatically.

'NO!' I shouted. 'Plan B has nothing to do with bees!'

Lenny stopped all the arm-waving and frowned. 'Why's it called *Plan Bee* then?'

'He has a point there, lassie,' Gregor said.

I took a breath to try and remain calm. 'He does *not* have a point!' I said through gritted teeth. 'There will be no bees in this operation!'

'But Plan Bee? The Bee Plan! It makes perfect sense!' Lenny said triumphantly.

'ENOUGH with the bees already!' I blared and Lenny and Gregor shot each other a look as if to say *I* was the one being unreasonable! 'Plan B is to see if we can find out *how* Ernie is planning to steal the Giant Ruby and stop him. The school trip is on Tuesday, which means we'll only have Monday to do it.'

'Gotta say, Lennster's Bee Plan sounds more excitin',' Gregor said.

'Exciting is not the word I'd use.'

Honestly, do you see what I have to work with?! I took another deep breath and continued.

'I propose we try Plan A and, if that fails, move on to Plan B.'

'And if that fails we'll go to the actual Bee Plan, involving actual bees!' Lenny said.

'Fine, we'll go to the Bee Plan,' I said, mainly to shut him up, but also because I didn't actually have a third option.

We'd just have to hope one of the first two worked. I would hate to see what Lenny would come up with if we got down as far as a Plan P.

CHAPTER 19

LENNY-IN-GREGOR'S-BODY

Gregor-in-my-body trotted off home from the mission-planning session at Agatha's with me curled up in my rucksack. I was beginning to worry that I'd slightly over-promised with my whole Bee Plan. I hadn't really thought through how I'd transport them all. I mean, Mum's got a lot of Tupperware, but I don't think even she has enough to contain a hundred thousand bees. I just had to hope that one of Agatha's more boring plans would work.

As soon as we opened the door of my house, I knew there was something different, probably because of my super-spy-detective senses. The house somehow felt fuller. Something about the air, or the smell of the place.

And then I heard his voice.

'Hello, son.'

Dad! Dad was here for a visit! I hadn't been sure if gargoyles had hearts, but they must do because one was certainly hammering in Gregor's stony chest. My dad was actually here! Finally, he must have had a break from being an international super-spy. And here I was, stuck in the body of a gargoyle, squeezed into my own school bag, with a pair of cheesy football socks tangled round my ears. Not ideal!

I peeked through the zip to see him better. His dark hair was parted to one side, he was perfectly shaven and grinning from ear to ear. Just like he always was.

'Give your dad a hug then!' he said to Gregor-in-my-body.

All I wanted to do was spring out of the bag and throw myself at him. To bury my face in his chest and be squished by his arms. But I didn't think finding out that his only child had turned into a gargoyle would be quite the father-son reunion he'd been looking for.

'Come on!' he said, arms open wide.

'Och, no thanks,' said Gregor-in-my-body. 'I'm no' really the huggin' type. Unless Mrs Tuchus – I mean Mammy – is around?'

I groaned. What does 'no' really the huggin' type' even mean? *Everyone* really loves hugging! Surely?

'Well, that's changed,' Dad said. 'You always used to love my hugs.'

I STILL DO! I wanted to shout.

But Gregor said, 'Aye – well, I'm no' the same as I used to be.'

'So I see. Is that a . . . *Scottish* accent?' My dad shot a beady look at Gregor-in-my-body.

'Aye,' said Gregor. 'All the rage at school at the moment. Everyone's doin' it.'

'Is that right?'

This was going wrong. My dad's super-spy brain had already worked out something was up! Stupid hug-hating Gregor was going to blow our cover!

'Get out!' I whispered urgently.

'I only just got here,' Dad said, looking hurt and confused.

Not you, I thought. *Us!* We needed to leave quickly. I gave Gregor a little kick and he got the message.

'Aye, well, I'll be off then, Daddy-o,' Gregor replied, and he ran upstairs with me jiggling and jumbling about inside my school bag.

From behind us, my dad called, 'I was going to teach you to ride that bike I got you for your birthday! I thought that's what you wanted?'

'Mebbe some other time, eh?' Gregor said.

But *when*? I thought. *When would this time come again?*

'Is everything OK, Lenny?' Dad shouted after me.

'Aye, Papa-T,' Gregor said. 'Everythin's fine!'

But everythin' wasn't fine. It wasn't fine at all.

I don't mind admitting that later I might have had a tiny cry as Gregor-in-my-body ate dinner downstairs with Dad, while I had to hide under my bed, praying that Gregor didn't slip up and start chewing the plates or something.

I couldn't believe it. I hadn't seen my dad in *ages*, and now I was going to miss my chance to be with him because I was a stupid gargoyle. It was horrible. He was so near, yet so far away. I knew when I signed up for the life of a spy-detective that it wouldn't always be an easy one, but this was the most difficult thing yet. I had to get back into my own body and soon.

That evening, Dad left to go back to his own flat without me even getting the chance to say goodbye. I watched him walk off down the street, with no idea when I'd see him next. He was bound to be busy again soon, doing important spying work and

saving the world. Sometimes I get the impression Agatha doesn't believe that my dad is an actual spy, just a sales rep like he pretends to be. But that just shows you how good he is and that her spy-detective senses aren't as hot as she thinks they are. I guess that's why she'll always be an assistant.

For the rest of the weekend, I had to listen to Gregor and Mum having fun while I was stuck in my bedroom. He helped her make dinner, did the hoovering *and* the washing-up, even sat and watched all her boring TV programmes with her. And when the most boring one of them all came on, the one about antiques, he was an absolute mega-show-off, telling her about the history of all the objects.

I did not like it *one bit*. It's not like I'm a huge fan of housework or old vases. But I am a fan of my mum. And she's *my* mum, not Gregor's. I couldn't wait to stop Ernie and Minerva so I could get back to being me. It's really no fun being a gargoyle. Especially one with such an itchy bum crack.

On Monday, I couldn't get back into my school bag quick enough. I was raring to go, although I wasn't sure how Agatha planned on telling Dr Errno that his best friend, Ms Stranglebum, had built a secret laboratory in his basement in order to run an international crime school.

'Easy,' she said as we walked through the gates.

'We'll just go right up and tell him. Now keep your head in that backpack, would you?'

She shoved me down and zipped the bag up, leaving just a little spyhole.

A few minutes later, I heard knocking and a shout of, 'Enter!' from Dr Errno.

He was sitting behind his desk. A beam of sunlight streamed through the window and bounced off his bald head. His black school gown was draped round him like bat's wings.

'Ah, Agatha Topps and Lennox Tuchus, what brings you to my office so early on this bright Monday morning? Registration isn't due to start for another hour.'

Agatha took a breath. 'Something important and very serious brings us here. Sir, we need to speak to you about Minerva Industries and this whole Pedal-Power thing –'

Dr Errno leaned forward. 'I know some pupils have struggled with the physical side of things –' he eyeballed Gregor-in-my-body – 'but I'm surprised at you, Agatha. You've been doing well rather well, haven't you?'

'I suppose I have, but, sir, it's not just about the pedalling. It's worse than that. We think that Ms Stranglebum – no, we don't think, we *know* that Ms Stranglebum has a plan to –'

'Improve the educational standards of Little Strangehaven Primary as well as reduce the school's carbon footprint and look after the well-being of the staff? Because that is what she's doing, Agatha, and I would be very careful about what you say next.'

Dr Errno's cavernous nostrils flared so wide I couldn't help but stare deeply into them. I've always thought they had hypnotic powers, and, even from the safety of my bag, they were sucking me in. All I could focus on was those seemingly infinite black holes. Eventually, and with immense effort, I managed to give myself a little slap round the face and pull myself out of the nostril-trance.

'Pamela Stranglebum has been nothing but a force for good in this school since she arrived and I won't hear a bad word said against her,' Dr Errno continued.

'But, sir, you're going to have to! She's built a laboratory in the basement and it's got these machines that increase intelligence by five hundred per cent and she's –'

'Agatha Topps, have you been in the basement? That is out of bounds to pupils! And I am well aware Ms Stranglebum is building a state-of-the-art laboratory down there. This school has been crying out for one for years. I also fail to see how increasing a child's intelligence by five hundred per cent is a bad thing.'

'It's a bad thing if that child uses it for evil!' Agatha said. 'Ernie Strewdel is –'

'Unrecognizable, I know. I mean, what a transformation!'

'But, sir, Ms Stranglebum is using him as an example –'

'And what a fine example he is!'

'Sir! YOU NEED TO LISTEN!'

'No, Miss Topps, *you* need to listen. You've already admitted to being in the basement without permission. If you continue with this nonsense about Ms Stranglebum, you will be banned from the museum trip tomorrow. Do I make myself clear?'

'Yes, sir,' Agatha said angrily but quietly.

'Tuchus? TUCHUS! Put my paperweight down immediately. That was a gift from Mummy and is not for licking!'

After Dr Errno had dismissed us, Agatha whispered into the bag, 'So, on to Plan B – follow Ernie and see if we can find out what he's up to.'

'And then source one thousand Tupperware boxes,' I said. 'For the *actual* Bee Plan . . .'

CHAPTER 20

AGATHA

We headed for the cloakroom. I hung my coat on my peg, then sat on a bench with Gregor-in-Lenny's-body, and Lenny in the bag at my feet.

'Honestly, what is it with grown-ups? They really are so unbelievably dumb sometimes. Ms Stranglebum has well and truly pulled the wool over Dr Errno's eyes.'

'Ooh, do you think she got it from the sheep-cat?' Lenny said from inside the rucksack.

'*What?* Are you getting enough air in there, Lenny?'

I looked down at him – his stony nose was poking out of the bag – and then over at Gregor, who was licking one of the coat pegs. My goodness, I was up against it with these two as assistants.

'It's a bit stuffy, but I'll soldier on.'

'Good, because we all need to have our spy-detective senses cranked up to the max. Ernie's going to try and steal the Giant Ruby tomorrow, which means we don't have long to figure out how to stop him. No way will Stranglebum be shooting down satellites with her evil ruby-laser, not on my watch! We need to have eyes on Ernest Strewdel at all times. ALL TIMES! Do I make myself clear?'

'*All times?*' Lenny said. 'What if he goes to the loo? I don't want my eyes anywhere near him then.'

'Aye, that's takin' it a wee bit far, lassie,' Gregor-in-Lenny's-body said.

'Nothing is too far for a professional spy-detective. I never said ours was a glamorous life, but we don't do it for the glamour. We do it for good. I have to know everything Ernie does!'

'Agatha –'

'Shush, Lenny, I'm talking. I need you both to pay attention. We can't let Ernie out of our sight –'

'But, Agatha –'

'Lenny, please shush! As I was saying, we have to be one hundred per cent focused on Ernie. We'll follow him at break and lunchtime and in between lessons. If he leaves class, one of us goes too –'

'AGATHA!' Lenny shouted, and started shuff-hoppling across the floor in his bag.

I grabbed the handle and held him up so I was looking him in the eyes.

'Lennox Tuchus, if you keep interrupting, I will be forced to zip you up and hang you on a peg for the rest of the day!'

'But, Agatha,' Lenny said, thrashing about, 'there he is! Ernie Strewdel! At the far end of the corridor. He's at school already!'

'Lenny! Why didn't you say anything sooner?'

'I tried! But you kept –'

'Shush, Lenny! No time.' I jumped up and slung him on my back. 'Right, follow me, Gregor. We're going to trail Ernie. Be super quiet and slink like you've never slinked before!'

Unfortunately, because Lenny had taken so

long to raise the alarm, Ernie had quite the head start on us. I speed-tiptoed down the corridor after him, making zero noise. I'd trail Ernest Strewdel like the master of espionage I was. A girl moving only in the shadows. Invisible, unseen, concealed from human eyes –

'ACHOOOOO!'

Except I couldn't be any of those things because I had an assistant capable of sabotaging even the simplest of plans.

Ernie spun round. 'Bless you.'

'Thank you,' Lenny said. FROM INSIDE THE BAG!

Ernie frowned, then looked at Gregor-in-Lenny's-body, then at my bag and frowned deeper. 'Did . . .?'

'Did what?' I said innocently.

He shook his head. 'Never mind. You two are in early.'

'So are you,' I pointed out. 'More Minerva training?'

'Something like that,' Ernie said. He checked his watch. 'Better get going.'

'OK,' I said as he started off down the corridor. 'Have a great day!'

When he turned the corner, I grabbed Lenny off my back and unzipped the bag. 'Right, we're going to trail him again,' I hissed, sticking my face inside. 'But can we have less of the sneezing and the talking, please, Lenny?'

'Or maybe we could have less of you sounding like an elephant wearing clogs!' he snapped back.

'Excuse me?!' I sounded nothing like an elephant wearing clogs.

'You're excused,' Lenny-in-Gregor's-body replied.

'That's not what I meant, Lennox Tuchus!'

'And I'm sure you didn't mean to be such a boomy-footed spy-detective either, but I forgive you.'

'*You forgive me?*'

'Yes, you can't help having such big feet. But,

Agatha, I really think we should focus on trailing Ernie.'

'ARGH! I KNOW THAT!!'

I grabbed Gregor-in-Lenny's-body by the arm and chased off down the corridor, which was not easy with Lenny-in-Gregor's-body bouncing about in his bag on my back and weighing an actual TONNE!

I turned the corner just in time to see Ernie heading into the library. I waited a second, to make sure he wasn't going to reappear, checked the vicinity for robot owls, and then scuttered up to the door. I pressed my eye to the keyhole.

'No good – the key's still in it. I can't see anything. What do we do now?'

I let Lenny out of the bag in the unlikely event that he might have an idea.

'Anyone got a plan? Lenny? Gregor?'

Lenny opened Gregor's mouth.

'Preferably one that doesn't involve a hundred thousand bees, that is.'

He shut it again.

But then he nodded at a tiny window high above the door.

'Why don't you climb up there and peek in?'

As far as Lenny ideas go, that wasn't bad.

'That's an excellent plan,' I said, to be encouraging. 'With one tiny change.'

'What?'

'*You* should climb up there.'

'Why me?'

'Because you're a gargoyle.'

'Only because *you* said we had to wait because it's too risky to change me back!'

'Which is true, and now also useful because gargoyles are designed to climb and –'

'Ah, technically, gargoyles are no' designed to climb,' interrupted Gregor-in-Lenny's-body very unhelpfully. 'We're designed to do a limited amount o' shimmyin' and then hang on to the side o' buildings. Fer a really long time. We're clingers more than climbers.'

'Well, do *you* want to climb up there?' I glared. 'Because it sounds like you're volunteering.'

'No, I cannae! This body has no strength whatsoever!' Gregor-in-Lenny's-body said.

'Excuse me!' Lenny-in-Gregor's-body shot back. 'My body is actually *extremely* strong for its small size. I'm like a dung beetle.'

I stamped my foot. We didn't have time for this!

'All right, elephant-clogs,' Lenny said.

'Enough of the elephant-clogs! Now, Lenny,' I said, quite forcefully, 'the fact of the matter is that, while you are a gargoyle, you're small and less likely to be seen. And, if anybody spots you, you can just freeze and they'll think you are an ordinary statue.' He couldn't argue with that logic. 'Now get up there before I throw you myself.'

With a lot of huffing and puffing and complaining, he finally shimmied up the frame of the door, did a flying jump and caught the window sill. He slowly peeked over it and through the window.

'What do you see?' I whispered.

'The library,' Lenny said triumphantly. 'Books. More books. Quite a lot of books actually.'

'I know what a library is. Can you see Ernie?'

'Ooh! Yes! He's with Ms Stranglebum. She's holding something . . . It's a robot owl.'

A robot owl? Interesting.

'What else do you see?'

'Now Ms Stranglebum's saying something. She's lifting the owl up. Crikey! She just fired a laser from the owl's eyes! It hit a book! The book's on fire! I don't think they've noticed. They're both laughing. She's handing the owl to Ernie. He's putting the owl in his bag. The book is still on fire . . . Stranglebum's telling him something else. Now Ernie's nodding. Now Stranglebum's nodding. Now they're both nodding. Now they're nodding and laughing. Now they're just laughing. Or maybe cackling. Yes, they're probably evil-cackling. That book is *really* burning now. They should probably do something about that.

But they're still cackling. Still cackling. Still
cackling . . . Oh, they've stopped. They've spotted
the fire. They're jumping on it to try and put it
out. It's not going out. More jumping . . . More
jumping . . . Some shouting. They're running
about in circles now. Oh, Stranglebum's grabbed a
jug of water. She's pouring it on the fire. It's gone
out. Stranglebum looks serious now. She's saying
something else. More nodding . . . Oh no . . .'

'Oh no, *what*?' I hissed up at him.

'Stranglebum's opening the door,' Lenny said after the door opened. 'Now they're stepping out into the corridor,' he said after they'd stepped out into the corridor.

CHAPTER 21

LENNY-IN-GREGOR'S-BODY

*B*ecause neither Agatha nor Gregor-in-my-body had listened to my very timely warnings that Ms Stranglebum and Ernie were leaving the library, they ended up standing face to face with them, with me dangling heroically above.

It was a very tense situation. One made tenser because the window frame to which I was clinging with my gnarly fingertips appeared to be crumbling under my weight.

Ms Stranglebum sniffed sharply, then pointed a very sharp, perfectly manicured finger at Agatha. 'What are you up to?'

'Just hanging around,' Agatha said innocently.

I felt one of my talons lose grip.

'Liar,' Ernie snapped back. 'You were spying on us, weren't you?'

Another talon came free.

Ms Stranglebum's eyes narrowed. 'Is that true?'

Then another talon. Which left me barely holding on with two.

'We weren't spying,' Agatha said, glaring at Ms Stranglebum.

'That's right – we were definitely no' listenin' to yer evil plannin',' Gregor-in-my-body added.

'Would you like me to tell you what happens to people who snoop?' Ms Stranglebum said, glaring straight back at Agatha.

'Och no, no' really,' Gregor said.

'Well, I'm going to,' Ms Stranglebum spat. 'And you're not going to like it one bit.'

She reached out and grabbed Agatha by the arm. 'You're coming with me!'

Which is when my fourth talon lost grip and I

plummeted towards the ground, wailing, 'I thought I had five!'

I hit something soft, and then something hard, but fortunately I had fallen head first, which protected the rest of me. I must have blacked out for a second or two because, when I opened my eyes, Agatha and Gregor were standing over me, wearing very proud expressions.

'Lenny, that was unbelievable!' Agatha said.

'What was?' I said, scrambling to my feet and wobbling about.

'The way you just took out both Stranglebum and Ernie!' Agatha said. 'It was amazing!'

Gregor-in-my-body gave Ms Stranglebum and Ernie, who were lying in a heap on the floor next to me, a little prod with his foot. 'They're oot cold!'

I scratched my head, then shrugged, then spun in a circle and said, 'I *am* amazing . . . but why am I here?'

'Excellent point!' Agatha said. 'We have to leave before they come round!' She grabbed my hand and charged down the corridor towards the broom cupboard. 'We need somewhere to talk in secret.'

It was very cramped and very dark in the broom cupboard.

'Now everybody be quiet and let me think . . .' Agatha said. 'What's that slurping noise?'

'Sorry, tasty broom handle,' Gregor-in-my-body said. 'I usually nibble when I'm nervous, but I cannae eat so I thought I'd lick.'

'I'm a bit dizzy-whizzy,' I said because I was.

Agatha grabbed me by my shoulders. 'Now is not the time to be dizzy-whizzy! I know how Ernie's planning to steal the ruby tomorrow. He's going to use that robot owl to –'

'Peck the museum security guards' eyes out so they can't see!' I said.

'The savagery o' those birds knows no bounds,' Gregor said, shaking my head.

Agatha blinked. 'Or here's an idea: he'll use the owl's laser eyes to short-circuit the video cameras and then cut through the impenetrable glass case and swipe the Giant Ruby!'

'Possible, but I think the eyeball-pecking is more likely.'

She sighed. 'No, Lenny. Just no. So what we need to do is –'

'GOGGLES!'

'What?'

'We need to give the security guards goggles! If they have goggles, their eyes won't be pecked out.'

'A fine idea!' Gregor said.

Agatha looked at me, then at Gregor-in-my-body, but didn't say anything. I think she was finally starting to realize where the real brains of this operation lay.

'Where could we get goggles from?' I said.

'The science lab?' Gregor suggested.

'Excellent! Great thinking!'

'NO!' Agatha suddenly roared. 'We don't need goggles! Or a hundred thousand bees or any other ridiculous thing you numpties come up with! We *need* to get that owl off him.'

'I suppose that could work too,' I said.

'Let's creep out now,' Agatha said. 'Grab it while Ernie's still unconscious.'

She opened the cupboard door and we headed back to the scene of my magnificent dive-bomb attack, but neither Ms Stranglebum nor Ernie were there.

'Dratballs!' Agatha said. 'They must have come round. We're going to have to try and get it off him in class.'

When we got to the classroom, Ernie was already pedalling away. From inside my school bag, I heard him say to Agatha, 'I don't know what just happened back then, but that will be the one and only time you get the better of me. I'm watching you, Agatha Topps.'

Agatha said, 'And I am watching *you*, Ernie Strewdel!' And she pointed at her eyes with two fingers and then back at him. I thought it was quite menacing, but he just laughed.

For the rest of the day, Agatha and Gregor-in-my-body tried to get Ernie's bag off him, but he did not let it out of his sight. He pedalled with it on his back. He ate lunch with it on his back. He even went for a wee with it on his back.

That evening, on our way home, Agatha said, 'We'll get it off him on the school bus on the way to the museum. Once we have that bird, even Ernie won't stand a chance. He might be Super-Ern, but there's three of us and only one of him. I'm sure we can do it. Minerva will be finished.'

The next morning, we met outside the school gates by the bus. Miss Happ ticked our names off as we arrived and made us put on a hi-vis vest that said *Property of Little Strangehaven Primary School* on it, and off we went on our owl-napping mission.

Now I'm absolutely certain that, if I hadn't been a gargoyle, the following events would have gone a LOT more smoothly. But it's very hard to be a saving-the-school-and-stopping-the-criminal-masterminds-super-spy-detective when you're made of rock and squished into a rucksack.

'Just stop moaning!' whispered Agatha as she clambered into her seat and dumped me and the rucksack by her feet. 'I should be the one moaning! Have you any idea how tiring it is lugging you about all day? You weigh an actual TONNE.'

Her mood didn't improve when I tried to explain to her a little later – as quietly and politely as possible – that the plan to stop Ernie had zero chance of success while I was stuck in the bag because I was the one with all the spy-detectivizing abilities and, without me, it was doomed to fail.

'Agatha, the plan to stop Ernie has zero chance of success while I'm stuck in this bag because I am the one with all the spy-detectivizing abilities and, without me, it is doomed to – OW! WHAT DID YOU DO THAT FOR?'

I rubbed my head. Agatha – at least I think it was her – had given me a sharp kick.

'Right,' Agatha whispered sternly, 'I'll show you! Come on, Gregor – let's do it!'

I unzipped the bag so I could peek out and watch the inevitable disaster unfold.

The plan was simple – because Agatha had come up with it. In my experience, her simple plans always failed spectacularly, but she would not listen to me when I pointed that out either.

Her idea was to distract Ernie, and then Gregor-in-my-body would steal Ernie's bag and throw it out of the bus window. But nobody – and certainly not super-brained Ernie – would fall for that. I did try to tell her.

Agatha quickly scuttled down the bus and snuck in behind Ernie and Jordan. Ernie's bag was on the floor under their seat.

Agatha popped her head over the headrest. 'Hello there, Ernie.'

'What do you want, Topps?' Ernie sneered. 'I'm busy.'

I miss the old Ernie. Before he got turned into a criminal mastermind, Ernie never sneered.

'I wanted to give you a chance to stop what

you're doing,' Agatha said, ignoring Ernie's sneer.

'I don't know what you're talking about.'

'I think you do,' Agatha continued. 'And I'm just letting you know that we *will* stop you, so you might want to think about just not trying it in the first place.'

'You? You and Lenny *Tuchus*? Don't make me laugh – you two losers can't stop me!'

New Ernie was SO awful.

'Oh my word, what's that?!' gasped Agatha suddenly, pointing outside.

Ernie swung round to look, and Gregor-in-my-body grabbed his bag and, before Ernie could do anything, stuffed it out of the window.

I was lost for words. Agatha's plan had actually worked. I couldn't believe 'super-genius' Ernie had fallen for the 'look over there' manoeuvre – the oldest trick in the book!

Instead of getting angry, though, Ernie just looked confused.

'Agatha,' he said, 'why did your loser friend just throw Jordan's bag out of the window?'

Agatha's face fell.

As did Jordan's. 'YOU DID WHAT?'

I mean, I'm not saying I was *happy* that the plan had failed without my help, but I'm also not saying I wasn't *un*happy I'd been proved right.

'YOU DID WHAT?!' screamed Jordan again.

Agatha didn't really answer that question, she just scuttled back to her seat.

'Don't say a word,' she hissed down to me.

Jordan was still shouting and screaming about his bag as we pulled up to the museum and everybody piled off the bus and into the exhibition.

All we could do now was follow Ernie,

desperately trying to anticipate his next move. He knew we were on to him, but didn't seem to care. Every time he turned a corner to find one of us there, he'd just grin and shake his head. Sometimes he even waved. It was like he *knew* we didn't stand a chance. But we wouldn't give up. We shuffled from room to room, never letting him out of our sight – which was difficult because it was half-price Tuesday for pensioners, and hordes of oldies were doddering about the place like handbag-clutching zombies.

We traipsed behind Ernie through an exhibit of Victorian lavatories, a collection of Roman treasure, and a room full of medieval weapons, including a model of a machine called a trebuchet, which is basically a giant catapult on wheels.

Finally, we shuffled into the room that contained the Giant Ruby of Kathmandu. It was dimly lit, spotlights shining on the twinkling jewel, which was slowly revolving beneath its impenetrable glass dome. Security guards stood against every wall. Cameras eyed the huge gemstone from every corner. Grannies sat on every seat, chuntering to each other and unwrapping tuna sandwiches.

Surely not even super-brain Ernie could pull this heist off with so many people around?

Turns out I was wrong. Super-brain Ernie *could* pull it off.

And he did.

Quick as a flash, he opened his bag, grabbed the robot owl and shot a single laser beam at a fire detector on the ceiling. Immediately, an alarm started blaring. Then the sprinklers opened up.

And that's when the chaos really began.

Trying to protect their hairdos with their soggy sarnies, the grannies were merciless in their rush to escape the downpour. The security guards,

who were already slipping around, were knocked off their feet by the horde of rampaging wrinklies. Walking sticks were brandished like clubs, Zimmer frames used as battering rams.

It was terrifyingly brutal – they were a force of nature.

Ernie was calm amid the mayhem. A few more blasts from the laser-eyed owl and he had knocked out all the security cameras.

I bounced around on Gregor-in-my-body's back as he and Agatha desperately tried to reach Ernie, but it was impossible. There were too many dripping grannies in the way.

I had to do something. I'd promised to stay in the bag – but I knew when I was needed. Desperate times call for a hero. And I was that boy. Or gargoyle.

I unzipped the bag, sprang out and rushed towards Ernie, my talons clacking over the marble floor.

One granny pointed at me, her mouth gaping in horror, and screamed, 'A . . . A MONKEY!!!'

This didn't help the situation. In fact, it made matters worse and sent the oldies even more frantic in their bid to escape the sprinklers and the monkey/gargoyle/me.

It was a whirl of chaos. And, amid this pandemonium, Ernie – cool as you like – slid out a pair of rocket boots from his bag and put them on. He then walked over to the ruby, pulled a little black disc from his pocket and placed it on the glass case. It beeped three times, then exploded. The dome shattered and I watched in despair as Ernie Strewdel calmly took hold of the Giant Ruby, activated his rocket boots and shot off towards the roof.

CHAPTER 22

AGATHA

On reflection – and I hate to admit it – I probably should have come up with a better plan than the bag-tossing idea. But, in my defence, all Lenny and Gregor were giving me were goggles and bees. Anyway, things had now become a lot more difficult than I'd imagined, what with all the old people getting in the way and the fact that Ernie was now airborne and we were very much ground-borne.

I ran over to a security guard, who was yelling at the pack of rampaging pensioners (who were screaming something about a monkey) to exit in an orderly fashion, and pointed upwards.

'That kid's stealing the ruby!'

The guard looked at the ceiling, where Ernie

had perched on a high beam, and said, 'Oh no, you don't!'

But, before he could do his security-guard thing, the robot-owl librarian blasted him full in the face with its laser eyes. The guard fell to his knees and screamed, 'I can't see! I'm blind!'

An old lady on a mobility scooter scooped him up, threw him over her lap and screeched away, shouting, 'Don't worry – the WI never leave a man behind!'

Lenny-in-Gregor's-body, who had released himself from the bag without permission, scuttled up to me and said, 'What did I tell you about needing goggles?'

'Now is not the time for I told you so's!' I shot back.

'You're right!' Lenny replied. 'Now's the time for *action*!'

'Well, go on then!' I said. 'Get active!'

Lenny started running on the spot, his tiny gargoyle legs a blur.

'Not that kind of active! *Sheesh!* What are we going to do now?'

The last of the crowd disappeared through the museum's double doors, followed by Gregor-in-Lenny's-body, who was shouting, 'Save yerselves! The end is nigh!' with a crazed look in his eyes. He would have run out too if I hadn't grabbed him by the collar of his hi-vis vest.

'Pull yourself together!' I shouted. 'We need to think fast. Ernie's still up there!'

'Not for long, losers!' Ernie called down to us, and let out an evil cackle.

'He's actually quite good at that,' Lenny said.

'Don't encourage him,' I replied.

'What *is* that thing?' Ernie said, gesturing to Lenny-in-Gregor's-body.

'That's Lenny. He got swapped into the body of a gargoyle in Stranglebum's evil lab.'

Ernie smirked. 'He got *what*?'

'It's not important,' I said.

'It is a bit important,' Lenny shot back.

I supposed it *was* a bit important, but not our biggest issue at that moment in time, so I shouted, 'Ernie, listen to me! We know everything! We know what Stranglebum has done to you! You don't have to be that person. You're not really evil! You're better than this! If she gets the Giant Ruby, she'll blast all the satellites from the sky and take over the world!'

Ernie's face changed and for a moment he almost looked sad. 'OK,' he said, 'I'll stop.'

I have to admit, I was surprised. But then I can be quite persuasive and I have studied a lot of negotiation techniques in spy-detective manuals.

'Really, Ernie? That's great! Really great!'

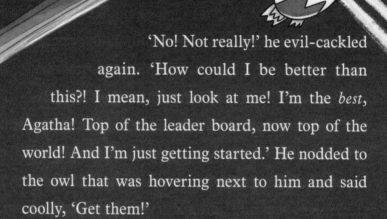

'No! Not really!' he evil-cackled again. 'How could I be better than this?! I mean, just look at me! I'm the *best*, Agatha! Top of the leader board, now top of the world! And I'm just getting started.' He nodded to the owl that was hovering next to him and said coolly, 'Get them!'

The owl turned its head in our direction. I only just had time to shout, 'Duck!' before it blasted us with its laser eyes.

To which both Lenny and Gregor shouted, 'Where?'

Because they would, wouldn't they?

'Not the feathery kind!' I shouted. But it was too late.

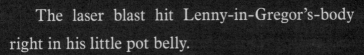

The laser blast hit Lenny-in-Gregor's-body right in his little pot belly.

'*Noooooooooooo!*' I shouted as he fell backwards. Not my Lenny!

Lenny didn't move. He just lay there.

'Lenny, Lenny, speak to me!' I scrambled over to him and took his hand. It was cold. But then it would be: he was made out of stone after all.

He still didn't move.

'Lenny! Please! Say something!'

'Something.'

OK, not quite what I'd meant, but it would do. Relief flooded through me and I flung my arms round his chunky little neck.

'Lenny Tuchus! You're OK! Well, you're still stuck in the body of a gargoyle, and we're being shot at by a crazed kid super-criminal, but apart from that you're OK!'

'Thank goodness! I thought the wee laddie was a goner fer sure!' Gregor-in-Lenny's-body said.

'But that laser's no match for extra-strong Scottish rock.'

Lenny grinned and then slid out from my arms and did quite an interesting victory belly dance until the owl shot him a second time.

'Duck!' I shouted.

Gregor-in-Lenny's-body and Lenny-in-Gregor's-body both shouted, 'Where?' again.

'Seriously?' I said, pulling them to safety behind a display cabinet as the owl fired off more shots.

'Why d'ye keep bringin' up ducks?' Gregor-in-Lenny's-body said. 'Ye know ma thoughts on feathery beasties. Ducks, pigeons, flamingos – they're all the same. Nasty wee creatures.'

'It shot me in the belly again.' Lenny-in-Gregor's-body stuck out his bottom lip. 'I don't think Ernie likes me that much. And after I complimented his evil cackling.'

It really is quite astounding how easily they can both be distracted mid-mission. Their lack of focus was staggering.

'Will you two just listen! I have an idea!'

'If it's about goggles, I think it's a bit late for that,' Lenny said.

'It's not about goggles!'

'Well, I hope it's no' got anythin' to do wi' ducks,' Gregor said.

'Of course it's got nothing to do with ducks! Why would it be about ducks?!'

'Ye tell me. Yer the one obsessed wi' 'em.'

'*ARGGGGHHHHHHH!* JUST WAIT HERE! Keep Ernie talking. I'm going to go and get the trebuchet!'

'What do you want with a trebuchet?' Lenny-in-Gregor's-body asked.

'I'm going to get all medieval on Ernie Strewdel, that's what.'

They both looked at me blankly. 'But wha' are ye gonna fire from it?' asked Gregor finally.

I looked over at Lenny-in-Gregor's-body. His little round form had been a perfect bowling ball when we defeated a pack of Transylvanian gargoyles on our last mission. It would do nicely for hurling out of a catapult.

Lenny grinned. 'What? Why are you looking at me like that? What is it?'

CHAPTER 23

LENNY-IN-GREGOR'S-BODY

Agatha, ignoring my question, barked, 'Just keep Ernie talking!' and then ran out of the room.

'So . . . *ermmmm* . . . how's the ole evil-doin' goin' then?' Gregor-in-my-body called to Ernie, who was swooping about in his rocket boots, cackling and banging on and on about being a super-genius.

'You think you can distract me with your ridiculous questions, Tuchus? Is that the best plan you have?'

'No! We have a better plan!' Gregor said. 'It's gonna knock yer socks off. You wait!'

'Well, *this* I have to see,' Ernie said and gave a hollow, mocking laugh as the robot owl settled on his shoulder. I have to admit, it looked even cooler than a monkey.

He stayed above us, hovering and laughing, until eventually his laugh died, and he was just sort of hovering awkwardly.

'Actually, I might just go,' he said finally, then turned to the owl and added, 'Ms Stranglebum, the mission is complete. The Giant Ruby of Kathmandu is secure.'

'Has Ms Stranglebum transmogrified into that robot owl?' I asked, surprised.

'No, you idiot!' Ernie said. 'The owl is live-streaming everything so that Ms Stranglebum and the others can monitor the mission. A mission that is now over!'

'Not yet, it isn't!'

Agatha burst in, wheeling the model catapult behind her. Unfortunately, she'd forgotten to bring anything to fire from it. Typical Agatha.

'Right, get in,' she said, looking at me and pointing at the trebuchet.

'Who get in?'

'You get in,' she said.

'Me get in? In where?'

'In THERE!'

'YOU WANT ME TO GET IN THE CATAPULT?'

Agatha had well and truly lost her mind if she thought she was firing me out of that thing.

'Yes! You're just big enough!'

'That's . . . sizeist!'

'This is ridiculous,' Ernie said. 'I'm off.' And he blasted in his rocket boots towards the doorway behind us.

'Lenny! He's going to get away! Just do it!'

I knew exactly what Agatha was really saying. What she actually meant was, 'Please, Lenny. Only you can save the day. We need a hero. I need you to be *my* hero.'

'OK, Agatha. I'm ready to be your hero,' I

said, and she gave me one of her impossible-to-read looks. In return, I gave her a smart salute, and clambered into the bowl of the catapult.

It turns out I wasn't *completely* ready to be a hero because, the second she set the catapult off, three things happened as I hurtled through the air at a bajillion miles an hour:

1. I screamed in terror.

2. I farted in terror.

3. I weed in terror.

Agatha's aim was perfect, and this was bad for Ernie for three reasons:

1. I hit Ernie full on – and if you've never been hit in mid-air by a stone gargoyle that has been launched from a medieval catapult, believe me, you don't want to be.

2. The moment of impact coincided with the terror-fart.

3. Ernie might have also been caught in a shower of my terror-widdle.

I clung to Ernie and our combined weight was too much for his rocket boots. We came crashing to the floor in a great heap. Unfortunately for Ernie, who was having a REALLY bad thirty seconds, he came down right on top of the robot owl, which was not a soft landing. And I landed

right on top of him, which can't have been much fun either. But what was EVEN WORSE for Ernie was that the Giant Ruby fell out of his pocket and skittered along the floor. I watched as Agatha dived forward and snatched it up.

She stood over Ernie, who was knocked out cold, and said, '*Now* this mission is over.' Which was pretty cool, but should have been my line because

I had been the courageous cannonball after all!

I got to my feet shakily because I was a bit dizzy-whizzy again. Then the next thing I knew, I was thrust back into my bag along with the Giant Ruby, hoisted on the back of Gregor-in-my-body, and the three of us were running out, leaving Ernie still groaning on the floor.

Outside the museum, the crowd of angry old people jostled with schoolchildren and panicking security guards. Agatha swung a left into an alley and Gregor and I followed.

'I can't believe we did it!' she whooped as Gregor dropped me to the floor. 'We stopped Ernie! WAHOO!'

I popped out of the bag and held up the Giant Ruby triumphantly.

'Aye!' cheered Gregor-in-my-body. 'You managed to steal the extremely precious ruby from the museum! Excellent thievery!'

'What do you mean?' gasped Agatha, snatching it out of my hands.

'Well, we have the Giant Ruby, don't we?'

'Well, yes, but we didn't steal –'

'And we didnae pay fer it?'

'Well, no, but we're not thieves! We were protecting it!'

'And I'm sure tha's exactly how the police will see it,' said Gregor, but in a way that made it sound more like the police were already hunting us down, probably with attack dogs and helicopters.

I climbed a couple of steps that led up to a side entrance of the museum, to gain enough height to glare Agatha in the eye rather than the belly button.

'I am NOT going to prison because of your stupid plan, Agatha Topps!'

'Nobody's going to prison!' Agatha said, but she didn't look very sure of herself. In fact, she looked like she might be sick.

'Agatha, I started this school year as a regular boy. Thanks to you, I am now a gargoyle and a thief! My report is going to be the worst yet!'

'It's not my fault you transmogrified yourself into a gargoyle! And we're not thieves. We're . . . temporary custodians of the world's most valuable and dangerous jewel. We're the good guys.'

'Yup, because good guys always take valuable jewels from museums wi'oot payin' fer 'em,' Gregor said.

Agatha shot him one of her darkest looks.

'Gregor, you're really not helping! Look, everything is going to be absolutely fine . . .'

Well, she was *very* wrong about that.

Everything suddenly became very not fine. Very *absolutely* not fine. And I think Agatha could really only blame her own lack of planning and foresight for what happened next.

And what happened next happened very quickly. So quickly I was too stunned to react with my usual heroism. Which was actually probably a good thing because it meant that, when a white van with a silver owl emblazoned on the side screeched to a halt next to us and two people jumped out, I froze in terror.

And looked like an *actual* stone gargoyle, which was a top-notch disguise. I think my subconscious must have known that. Well done, super-subconscious!

From my statue-like position, I watched in horror as the two men wearing boiler suits (one of

whom looked a lot like Mr Whip because it *was* Mr Whip) bundled Agatha and Gregor-in-my-body into two big sacks, threw them into the back of the van and drove off.

Leaving me all on my own.

Very inconsiderate of Agatha.

It looked like it was down to me to save the day. *Again*.

CHAPTER 24
AGATHA

It was a bit of a surprise to suddenly find myself in the back of a van, being flung about like a sack of potatoes. A surprise that would not have happened if Lenny and Gregor hadn't delayed our getaway with all their ridiculous talk of us being criminals.

Clearly, Ms Stranglebum had been watching the events at the museum by owl-stream and had decided to take matters into her own hands.

'Gregor,' I hissed, 'are you OK?'

'Aye, why wouldnae I be?'

'Because we've been kidnapped.'

'Och, worse things happen on rooftops. And besides, I'm a gargoyle, I cannae be kidnapped. If anythin', I've been gargoyle-napped.'

Honestly.

'So what are we going to do?'

'Well, if I had ma own gnashers, I'd have chewed us oot o' here by now.'

'OK, any suggestions that don't involve eating large quantities of hessian sacking?'

'When they stop and open the doors, I say we attack.'

'Attack? We're inside thick hessian sacks. How are we going to attack from inside them?'

'Wi' bravery, wi' the hearts o' clansmen, wi' the hearts o' lions. Fer we may be bound, but our hearts are free! We must have the courage to follow them! We must battle –'

'Gregor, you're saying a lot of words right now, and none of them actually constitute a plan.'

'Well, have *you* got any ideas, Little Miss Negativity?'

'I'm just thinking of one, actually,' I said.

'So wha' is it?'

'Well –'

I didn't finish that sentence because: one, I didn't have an idea; and two, the van came to an abrupt stop and the back doors were flung open.

And that's when I heard myself cry, 'Attack!', which was a surprise.

Gregor shouted, 'Tha's the spirit, lassie!'

Then I heard some scuffling and a yell of, '*FREEEEDOM!*'

Spurred on, and with adrenaline pumping, I threw myself forward, hoping that the element of surprise might be on our side.

It wasn't.

I'd misjudged where the doors were and ran into the wall of the van so hard I bounced off it and landed on something with a thud.

The something made an *oooff* sound, then said, 'I didnae mean fer ye to attack me, ye eejit!'

Then I heard some sniggering.

That annoyed me. Kidnapping is a terrible profession. Kidnappers should treat it seriously. There should be no sniggering. I wiggled and flailed around until I managed to get to my feet.

'I demand you release us,' I said in my most authoritative voice.

'We're over here,' came a reply.

Oh.

I shuffled round. 'I demand you release us,' I said with slightly less authority.

'No can do, I'm afraid. We only follow one person's orders and that person is very keen to talk to you.'

And then, before I could reply, I was swooped over someone's shoulder, lifted out of the van and carried up some steps. A moment later, I heard a door creak open.

'Gregor!' I shouted. I didn't want to be carried off on my own, even if I am incredibly brave.

'Wha'?'

'I was checking you were still there.'

'No, I'm on a plane to the Maldives. Course I'm still here.'

'Will you two pipe down!' a familiar voice said.

'Will you two let us go?' Gregor replied.

'No!' said the familiar voice.

'Then in that case we'll bellow our lungs clean oot o' our bellies!'

And we did, all the way through several long corridors, down some steps, through a set of doors and then another, until finally we were dumped on the floor and the sacks were untied.

'Mr Whip!' I gasped, blinking as my eyes adjusted to the light. Impossibly, his shorts looked

even shorter, his legs poking out like an ostrich.

'Surprise!'

He stepped to one side to reveal Ms Stranglebum seated at the end of her long white oval table, her fingers steepled under her chin.

'Ah, there you are, my beauty,' she said.

It wasn't the welcome I'd been expecting from my captor.

'You can keep your compliments, Pamela,' I said, feeling extra powerful at using her first name.

'For I may be a beauty, but you are an evil, evil woman!'

She pointed to my hand. 'I meant the Giant Ruby.'

That was a bit embarrassing, to be honest.

'I knew that!' I said. 'But you're not having it!'

'Oh, I think you'll find I am.' Her voice was warm and treacly, like . . . well, treacle. 'For who's going to stop me? You're outnumbered.'

She glanced at Mr Whip, then at Ernie, who I was a bit surprised to see – they must have scooped him up off the museum floor. She then gestured to all the **TERRIBLE EVIL CRIME BOSSES**, who were seated round the table, and then at the crime boss's monkey. Finally, her cold eyes settled on me.

'No one saw what happened to you. No one is coming to help.'

But that wasn't true. Lenny Tuchus had.

It was then that the full magnitude of the situation dawned on me. I glanced over at Gregor.

He shrugged, then pulled a face, then shrugged again.

Only Lenny could save us.

Not the most brilliant news.

In fact, I think you'll understand why, at that point, I was 99.9999998 per cent convinced that we were doomed.

CHAPTER 25

LENNY-IN-GREGOR'S-BODY

It was time for me to strap on my big-gargoyle boots and save the day.

To rescue Agatha and Gregor-in-my-body, first I had to get back to the laboratory, which was not easy, what with me being a real-life gargoyle. Every time anybody came near me, I had to freeze like a statue because people don't expect to see a gargoyle walking down the high street, whistling a merry tune.

Yes, I'd realized I could whistle at last – probably because of Gregor's stone lips. But then I realized that whistling a merry tune was going to give me away, so I stopped, became immediately much better at sneaking and freezing like a statue, and was completely and totally successful apart from two tiny incidents with:

1. A toddler who kept pulling my ears, so I told him I'd bite his nose off if he didn't stop. He ran off screaming, which is understandable considering a statue had just come to life and threatened him with nose-munching violence.

2. A small granny who was convinced I was a lost dog called Mabel. When she tried to put a collar on me and lift me into her basket, I had to politely tell her I was not, in fact, a lost dog called Mabel. She also ran off screaming– again, understandably.

Once I made it to school, it was a bit easier to sneak about. I scuttled up the wall, across the roof, back down to the ground, in through the window,

made a quick stop-off at the toilet for an emergency poo (turns out gargoyle poos are made of stone and it shattered the toilet bowl and *might* have caused a small flood), then went down the staircase to the basement.

Basically, I was being a maximum, total, one hundred per cent friend-and-world-saving spy-detective.

Annoyingly, the door to the basement was jammed – no matter how much I pulled it, it wouldn't open. And then I heard the sound of footsteps walking down the stairs behind me! I was trapped!

I stood in the corner by the door and held my breath.

After two seconds, I had to let my breath out

because I wasn't very good at holding it, which is one of the two reasons I don't have my twenty-five-metre swimming badge yet (the other being my mortal fear of piranhas).

Instead, I opted for breathing as lightly as possible. The footsteps got louder and louder until Mr Whip appeared.

What was *he* doing here?

He didn't notice me, which was good, until he stubbed his toe on my foot. I let out a tiny yelp and Mr Whip bent over and peered at me with boogly, suspicious eyes.

I tried to stay as still as possible, which was difficult because I was only centimetres from Mr Whip's tiny shorts.

Eventually, the suspicion left his eyes and he rubbed his toe.

'Who on earth left this thing here?' he muttered to himself, picked me up, and pushed open the basement door (which I must have loosened).

The laboratory seemed deserted and Mr Whip

dumped me in the corner next to a cupboard. I watched as he trotted off to the door that led to the Minerva conference room. As soon as he was out of sight, I sprang into action.

I hurried across the lab, clocking that the Pedal-Power battery was fully charged, and just managed to stop the door from closing behind Mr Whip. As quietly as I could, I snuck down the corridor after him.

I peered through the conference-room window and, sure enough, there was Ms Stranglebum sitting at the oval table with all the **TERRIBLE EVIL CRIME BOSSES**, this time in person! And there in the corner of the room, tied up, were Agatha and Gregor-in-my-body. Ernie was standing next to them, staring at his feet.

Ms Stranglebum held up the Giant Ruby, a look of triumph on her face.

'As promised! The Giant Ruby of Kathmandu. So flawless it can focus laser beams until they are strong enough to slice through the moon, and shoot down all satellites not registered to Minerva Industries! I trust our demonstration has filled you with confidence about becoming part of the Minerva family, the most powerful criminal outfit on the planet?'

The **TERRIBLE EVIL CRIME BOSSES** all nodded.

'And speaking of the Minerva family, I have the next two Minor Menaces™ here ready for transformation. All it takes is a couple of minutes in the Neuron Accelerator™ and a few jolts from the Corruption Contraption™!'

At that, Agatha and Gregor-in-my-body struggled *unbravely* in their ropes, panic in their eyes. I don't think my face had ever been panicky before, and I did not like seeing it one little bit.

'But don't worry,' Ms Stranglebum continued. 'There are plenty of children to go around. I've been speaking to school heads all over the country, and every one is keen for their pupils to start pedalling for a "greener" future under the Pedal-

Power initiative! If you join Minerva today, by next week you too can have your own school full of criminal masterminds!'

All the **TERRIBLE EVIL CRIME BOSSES** grinned.

'So, who would like to see me transform these two now?' Ms Stranglebum pointed at Agatha and Gregor-in-my-body, who struggled even more. 'One of you could even take them away with you today!'

I had to do something! But *what*?

I squeezed my eyes shut and strained to think the cleverest thoughts possible, but, to my horror, nothing came into my usually brilliant brain.

I *always* had a plan, but this time I couldn't think of anything. Not a sausage.

And then it hit me – an idea so brilliant only *my* brain could have come up with it. If I couldn't think of a plan, I needed to make my brain better – over five hundred per cent better!

I had to get to the Neuron Accelerator™ – and fast!

I snuck back down the corridor, trying to stop my talons clacking on the floor, and into the laboratory.

A moment later, I placed the metal helmet on my head, ready to improve my brain!

But then I hesitated. If I used the energy on making myself 500 per cent more cleverer, there might not be enough left to swap me and Gregor back!

I shook my head. I knew what I had to do, no matter the cost. Agatha and Gregor needed me.

I switched the dial up to maximum – might as well go for it – and pressed the start button.

Nothing. I looked over at the big battery. The light flashed green – **100%**. There was enough power then. What was wrong? Maybe it wasn't working because my brain was *already* powered to the maximum!

And then I felt it.

A fizzing in my head. Jumbles of flashing images in my mind. A million thoughts began crashing round my brain, and yet I felt calm, confident and somehow empty of all self-doubt.

It had worked.

I was a genius!

A genius stuck in the body of a gargoyle, but a genius all the same! It was quite weird when you think about it, so I decided not to think about it any more.

And that was good because I could turn my newfound genius brain to the most urgent problem: how to save the day.

CHAPTER 26
AGATHA

The evil crime boss in the pinstripe suit looked me and Gregor-in-Lenny's-body up and down.

'Do they take much caring for?' she asked.

'They're very self-sufficient,' Ms Stranglebum said.

'Toilet-trained, I presume?' said massive-moustache-and-eyebrows man.

'Of course we're toilet-trained!' I snapped back, although maybe I shouldn't have done. Perhaps they'd have been less keen to buy us if they thought they'd be mopping up our whoopsies.

'And how are they with monkeys?' the crime boss with the monkey asked.

'They get on with monkeys brilliantly,'

Ms Stranglebum replied. 'With the Corruption Contraption™, we can program them to be utterly obedient, so their behaviour will be exemplary. Well, it'll be highly criminal, but you know what I mean – they will be at your command.'

'So they'll do whatever we want?' the lady boss asked.

'Whatever you want,' Ms Stranglebum confirmed. 'You've seen it yourself. I told Ernie to get the Giant Ruby, and he got it.'

The **TERRIBLE EVIL CRIME BOSSES** all nodded in agreement.

'So how much are we talking?' Monkey-Boss asked.

'To buy a Minerva franchise, including your own crime laboratory and all the necessary crime gizmos, is a million pounds up front, then a fifteen per cent cut of all your ill-gotten gains thereafter.'

'So if I wanted to take a kid today – there's a Picasso painting I'm planning to swipe next week – how much would that set me back?'

said Moustache-and-Eyebrows.

'Thirty thousand pounds,' said Ms Stranglebum promptly. 'Or forty-five thousand for the pair.'

'Excuse me!' I spluttered. 'That doesn't sound anywhere near enough! He'll make his money back immediately when he nicks that painting!'

'That may be so,' Ms Stranglebum continued, 'but I'm a businesswoman, and it's all about the long game. Every successful crime committed by a Minerva family member benefits us all.'

'Even so, you can definitely get more for me than thirty thousand measly pounds! I'd make an excellent child criminal. Way better than Ernie, at any rate. No offence, Ern.'

And yes, I realize that I shouldn't have been arguing over my own price tag, but that amount was, frankly, insulting.

Ms Stranglebum ignored me and turned back to the table of **TERRIBLE EVIL CRIME BOSSES**. 'Do I have any takers?

Monkey-Boss said, 'Go on then, I'll have one.'

Then he pointed at me. 'Not her, though. She's a bit too mouthy.'

'I AM NOT *MOUTHY*!' I yelled, then clamped my hand over my mouth.

Ms Stranglebum sighed. 'I'll tell you what, I'll throw her in for free with the boy.'

Seriously, what?! If I was going to be forced into a life of crime, it was most certainly not going to be as part of a buy-one-get-one-free offer!

Ms Stranglebum pushed a button and from the centre of the table rose something that looked like a dentist's chair, with added wires, and arm and leg restraints. I did not like the look of it one bit.

'The Corruption Contraption™!' she announced grandly. 'Mr Whip, bring the girl.'

Mr Whip strode over and dragged me towards the Corruption Contraption™. I tried to fight, but he forced me into the seat and strapped me in.

'Let me go!' I shouted.

'Er, no,' Ms Stranglebum replied, which I suppose was to be expected.

I looked over at Gregor-in-Lenny's-body, hoping that he might offer some help. But he seemed distracted. I was about to have a go at him for losing focus during a mission *again* when I noticed what he was looking at through the window.

Lenny-in-Gregor's-body pointing a bazooka at his own face.

I had to blink a few times to check. But yes, Lenny was about to shoot himself right between the eyes.

I was lost. If he was going to bazooka someone, surely it should be Ms Stranglebum? I thought

maybe he'd forgotten which was the right end, and was about to shout, '*NOOOOOO*, boulder-head!', but then I realized what he was doing.

It was the instant-camouflage bazooka! He was planning to sneak in undetected!

Which was possibly brilliant!

Or not.

Lenny fired. The power of the blast sent him flying backwards and I stifled a gasp. For a moment, I thought he'd knocked himself out, but then he jumped up, looking pretty pleased with himself. He was covered in a green Lycra bodysuit, complete with leaves and what looked like a stuffed parrot.

He'd shot himself with the jungle setting . . .

But that didn't seem to faze him because he suddenly rocketed upwards, flames coming out of his soles. It took me a moment to figure out what was going on, but then I remembered – the rocket boots! Honestly, I could not believe what my eyeballs were seeing.

Gregor and I watched, openmouthed, as Lenny careered round the corridor, turning somersaults and bouncing off walls and the ceiling and the floor, shedding leaves as he went, as he tried to work out how to operate the boots. Maybe I *should* have let him have a practice that first time we were in the lab together.

Eventually, though, he got them under control – well, *kind of* under control. He put one knobbly arm out, Superman-style, and in the other he scooped up a load of Minerva crime gizmos. Then he powered forward towards the door.

My heart leaped into my mouth, then bounced back down to my stomach, then ricocheted back into my mouth again.

He was doing it! Lenny Tuchus was going to save the day!

CHAPTER 27

LENNY-IN-GREGOR'S-BODY

Not everybody is a natural hero.

Some people just don't have it in them. And that's fine.

But every so often, when the world needs a hero, somebody steps up.

And today that person was Lennox T. Tuchus.

I had never felt more heroic as I blasted forward to save my two best friends.

I should have blasted the door open, but I didn't have total control of the rocket boots yet, and so I blasted more *through* the door, smashed into the frame, and fell to the floor in the centre of the conference room, my head reeling. I sat up and everybody –

Agatha, Gregor-in-my-body, Ernie, Ms Stranglebum, Mr Whip in his tiny shorts, all the **TERRIBLE EVIL CRIME BOSSES** and one monkey – was staring at me, open-mouthed at my heroic entrance.

'Is that . . . a flying *bush*?' one of the bosses asked.

'No! It's a gargoyle! It's Lenny Tuchus!' Ernie shouted.

I blasted up into the air again.

'You bet your backside it is,' I said.

'Why's it wearing a green leotard?' the lady crime boss asked.

'It's camouflage,' I replied.

She frowned. 'I don't think it is.'

'Never mind that! Get him!' Mr Whip jumped up and tried to grab my foot, but I blasted away from his clutches.

Straight into the wall.

'I'm OK!' I shouted to Agatha and Gregor-in-my-body, who were looking on in awe at my awesomeness.

Mr Whip leaped on to the table and had another

go at catching me, but I zoomed past him.

Into the other wall.

'I'm still OK!' I shouted as I bounced off.

'Don't just sit there!' Ms Stranglebum screeched. 'Get hold of that . . . that . . . thing!'

For a moment, the **TERRIBLE EVIL CRIME BOSSES** didn't move (I don't think they were too keen on the idea of chasing a flying gargoyle), but then Stranglebum really started shouting and they all jumped up.

I immediately took evasive action, which involved a lot more wall-bouncing and a couple of unexpected but very impressive somersaults.

Eventually, after I'd ricocheted off pretty much every surface in the conference room, barely escaping the grasping hands of a shoal of crime bosses and a monkey, I finally found my balance. I swooped above their heads, centimetres from their grabby fingers, whooping with laughter.

'You'll regret the day you ever crossed paths with Lennox T. Tuchus!' I cackled.

'Has he already been corrupted?' one of the crime bosses asked.

I flew over to Agatha, quickly released her from the restraints and handed her the stun gun.

'Spare nobody, faithful assistant!' I said, then blasted over and untied Gregor-in-my-body. 'Here! Catch!' I shouted and dropped the Wind-Blaster™ by his feet.

He looked at it in disgust. 'Wind-Blaster™? You didnae think o' pickin' up the Shrink-Your-Enemy-To-Amoeba-Size spray™ right next to it, laddie? Wha' am I

supposed to do wi' this – blow-dry their hair?'

I admit the Shrink-Your-Enemy-To-Amoeba-Size spray™ might have been a better idea, but sometimes heroes don't think: they just act.

And now was the time to act again.

I flew down and snatched the Giant Ruby off the table, and soared back into the air.

I held it aloft, triumphant.

'He who laughs last laughs longest!' I whooped, and then laughed for a really long time just to prove my point.

'Are you OK, Lenny?' Agatha asked, her face full of concern.

'Yes! It's just my new genius brain!' I said, tapping my forehead and winking at her, but using both eyes because sometimes even heroes can't wink with just one.

'Well, genius, we shall indeed see who laughs last!' Ms Stranglebum laughed, but not for as long as my laugh, and then she pressed a button on the table.

Hovering menacingly up from behind her, a flock gathered, their red eyes flashing, like an army of evil, mechanical flying soldiers, but instead of mechanical soldiers they were mechanical librarian owls.

'Uh-oh,' I said.

'Get him!' Stranglebum hissed, pointing at me. 'And my ruby!'

Their eyes turned to me as one. Then they started blasting their lasers, and chaos broke out.

The owls flapped after me, beaks hooting and lasers shooting in all directions. I flew about in zigzags so they couldn't lock their beams on to me.

Agatha finally sprang into action and began shooting the owls with her stun gun, but it didn't seem to work; they seemed unstunnable! So she blasted the **TERRIBLE EVIL CRIME BOSSES** instead.

Then one of the owls caught me with a lucky laser shot to my right foot! Fortunately, I was not injured, but *un*fortunately I now only had one working rocket boot. And that made steering rather difficult.

In fact, it made it completely impossible, even for a genius hero. I spun round the room, wildly out of control, ricocheting off the walls and the ceiling.

But actually that turned out to be a master stroke because the owls found it impossible to track my uncontrollable flight path, and began blasting wildly. But instead of hitting me they were zapping each other!

Those that weren't shot down swivelled their heads round violently, trying to get a fix on me. So violently, in fact, that their heads popped off! First one. Then another. Then all of them. Owl heads were pinging all over the place like corks from

champagne bottles! Without them, the owls could no longer navigate and crashed into each other. It was carnage!

'*NOOOO!*' screamed Ms Stranglebum. 'Somebody stop him! Get my ruby!'

It wasn't *somebody* that tried to stop me, though, but *something*.

That darn monkey!

It sprang on to my back. I spun round wildly, trying to shake it off, but the monkey held on tight to my ears.

I knew I couldn't have trusted that furry sidekick! Never trust a crime boss's monkey – *that* should be the first thing you learn at spy-detective school. Not all that slinking around and saying nothing business Agatha is always banging on about.

Anyway, I was spinning out of control with a screeching monkey on my back; even for a genius hero, this was intolerable. Then the monkey clambered forward to try to snatch the Giant Ruby.

'*Gerroff!*' I shouted as it wrapped its legs round my neck.

Agatha, who was still blasting **TERRIBLE EVIL CRIME BOSSES** with the stun gun, finally noticed what was going on.

'The ruby!' she shouted. 'Throw it to me!'

So I flung it at her, and that meant I could get the cheek-scratching, ear-biting monkey off my back. It was clinging on for dear life, shrieking and most definitely regretting its decision to jump on a gargoyle-boy with broken rocket boots hurtling round a room like an angry bluebottle.

Then Gregor-in-my-body stepped forward and started firing the Wind-Blaster™.

'Feel the force o' ma hurricane, ye bunch o' numpty-dumpties!'

We braced ourselves for a storm.

Nothing. Not even a puff of wind.

'Blasted blaster doesnae even work!' Gregor said, bashing the gun.

But it did work, just not quite how we'd imagined.

One of the crime bosses, a huge man in a suit with a square block of a head, suddenly let out the almightiest burp. He gasped and his hands shot to his mouth in surprise. Then the boss next to him, a short man with spiky

hair, let out an even bigger burp.

'Forget wha' I said – this thing works just fine.' Gregor-in-my-body grinned, then pointed the Wind-Blaster™ at Ms Stranglebum.

She held up her hands and cried, 'No!'

Gregor shot.

For a moment, nothing happened. But then Ms Stranglebum began trembling, her eyes crossed and her face went a deep red. She grabbed hold of the table to steady herself, and then let out the loudest, sloppiest fart my ears had ever heard.

The whole room was stunned into silence.

Then she clutched her bottom and wailed, 'Not again!', and another bottom blast pulsed through the room.

Gregor looked at his gun. 'A mighty fine weapon this has turned oot to be!'

He was right too. Soon every single criminal in the room was burping and farting, in between screaming and running around, trying to catch Gregor-in-my-body.

Ms Stranglebum staggered towards Agatha, shouting, 'Give me that – *burrppppppppppp!* – ruby!'

Agatha threw it to me and I caught it in mid-air. The monkey scrambled to try and get it, but I flung it to Gregor-in-my-body, who grabbed it just as a beefy criminal barged into him. Gregor made use of my excellent throwing arm and hurled it back towards Agatha.

Agatha skidded underneath it, made the catch, then was up and running straight out of the conference room. Ms Stranglebum chased after her, shouting and burping and farting.

I had to help Agatha, and, even though I was close to choking to death on the noxious fumes from all the **TERRIBLE EVIL CRIME BOSSES**, I valiantly flew after her. Somehow I managed to make it down the corridor, the monkey biting my ears all the way.

I crash-landed in the laboratory, and somersaulted along the floor. The monkey flipped off my back, flew through the air and landed smack-bang in one of the transmogrifier pods. Quick as a flash, Agatha slammed the door shut, trapping it inside. Then she ran towards me yelling, 'Lenny, are you OK?'

I didn't answer because my new genius brain was too busy coming up with yet *another* genius plan. It all came to me so clearly – the monkey, the Giant Ruby, Ms Stranglebum.

I curled myself up into a gargoyle ball and launched myself at Agatha. She'd understand in the end. As I rolled towards her, her expression changed from concern to confusion.

I angled myself just right.

She went head first straight over me, yelling, '*WHY?!*', and the Giant Ruby flew out of her hand.

Straight into the other transmogrifier pod.

And Ms Stranglebum jumped right in after it.

It was her turn to raise her fist, her eyes gleaming with triumph.

'Ha! Ha! The ruby is mine!'

But not for long.

I slammed the door shut and locked it. A look of horror crossed Stranglebum's face as it dawned on her what I was about to do.

With a stony fist, I hit the transmogrify button. Then I turned to Agatha.

'*That's* why.'

CHAPTER 28
AGATHA

As we both watched the Transmogrification Chambers™ begin to hum and judder into life, I only just managed to stop myself from walloping Lenny-in-Gregor's-body.

'You could have just told me to throw the Giant Ruby in there! Did you really need to boulder into me?!'

'My genius brain calculated that there wouldn't be time for your inferior brain to process the instruction and act accordingly.'

I found that highly unlikely so I frowned. 'You calculated?'

'Yup! And it turned out all right in the end!'

I sniffed, crossed my arms and turned my attention back to Ms Stranglebum. 'I'm not one hundred per cent happy with you right now, Lenny.'

Gregor-in-Lenny's-body strolled into the room, with both the stun gun and Wind-Blaster™ cocked under his arms. He nodded to the Transmogrification Chambers™. 'Wha's goin' on in there?'

Ms Stranglebum banged both fists on the pod window.

'LET ME OUT!' she cried. Then made an *oooo-oo-ah-ah* monkey noise. That put the willies up her and she hammered on the window even more frantically.

'I thought she might like a go in one of her own inventions,' Lenny-in-Gregor's-body said.

Ms Stranglebum began screeching for her evil boss pals.

'Help me, you halfwits!' she yelled. Then she stopped for a moment, picked something out of her hair and ate it.

'Ye won't be gettin' any help from them,' Gregor said. 'I've stunned every last one of 'em! Even got that PE teacher midway through a humongous bahookie belch!'

I looked back down the corridor and, sure enough, among the stunned boss bodies strewn about the floor, Mr Whip was bent over, his face frozen in a grimace and his hands on his knees. He was completely motionless and had a massive tear in the back of his too-tight shorts.

'Excellent job, Gregor,' I said. 'I'm afraid it's just you and the monkey now, Ms Stranglebum.'

'Hey!' Lenny-in-Gregor's-body said. 'Why does he get *excellent job* and I get *not one hundred per cent happy with you right now*? I was the one who saved the day.'

'Do you think we could discuss this later? It's just I'm a bit busy watching our latest nemesis transmogrify into a monkey.'

Ms Stranglebum let out another wail of, '*Noooooooooo-oooh-ooh-ahh-ah!*' and then scratched her armpits.

'See how you like it, being turned into something you're not!' Lenny-in-Gregor's-body said, pointing at his stony figure.

Ms Stranglebum tilted her head in confusion. It was clear her mind had almost completely left her body. Doubt rippled through me. 'Do you think we should really be doing this?'

'Wha' d'ye mean, lassie?' Gregor-in-Lenny's-body asked.

'If we transmogrify her into a monkey, won't we be no better than her?'

We all three looked at each other, then said, '*Nah!*'

'She'll struggle to rule the world as a monkey,' Lenny-in-Gregor's-body said. 'This is the safest way.'

And I had to agree with him.

The machine stopped humming and juddering and fell silent.

'I think it's done,' I said.

Cautiously, we walked over to the pod containing Pamela-in-a-primate's-body and peered in. I've never seen a grumpier-looking monkey in all my life.

'Has it worked? Is it her?' Lenny asked.

The grumpy monkey shook a fist at us. 'You won't get away with this, you horrible children!'

'That's her all right,' I said.

'We've done it,' Lenny-in-Gregor's-body said. 'Thanks to my super-brain, we've saved the world. Again!' Then he started singing, 'Go, me and my super-brain – Tuchus saves the world again!' and proceeded to do a celebratory dance that involved far too much bum-wiggling in my opinion.

'NOT. SO. FAST.'

Lenny stopped his bum-wiggling and we all turned and gasped. Somebody stepped into the lab.

'Ernie!' We all gasped again.

'Yes, it is I – *BURPPP!* – Ernie!' said Ernie.

He really *had* gone to the dark side if he was referring to himself in the third person.

'Seems you missed one, Gregor. Not so excellent now, is he, *Agatha*?' Lenny said.

'Really not the time, Lenny.'

'Let the evil monkey-lady go free. She's mine now,' Ernie demanded, then burped and farted, which sort of took the power out of his demand.

Emboldened, I took a step towards him. 'Who's going to make me?'

'Me and my genius brain,' Ernie said, and picked up the Shrink-Your-Enemy-to-Amoeba-Size spray™. 'Oh, and this.'

He pointed it at me.

'Shoot her!' Pamela-Monkey screeched.

'You wouldn't,' I said. 'You don't have it in you.'

Ernie's hand wavered a little. 'Just let her out, all right, Agatha? Why do you always have to be so . . . so . . . Agatha-ish?!'

I caught Lenny-in-Gregor's-body nodding in agreement and elbowed him. 'Oi, you!'

I glared at Ernie. '*Agatha-ish*? What even is that?'

'Well, it's when you get a bit –'

'I wasn't asking YOU, Lennox Tuchus!' I said, and elbowed him again.

'Shut up, you – *BURP!* – two! Just give me my monkey and the Giant Ruby and I'll get out of here.'

I REALLY did not like this new Ernie, but I liked the thought of being shrunk to an amoeba even less.

'What do you want Stranglebum and the ruby for anyway?' I asked.

He seemed to like my question because he smiled and started strolling round the laboratory. Evil villains always love to show off about their plans – trust me on this: I have experience.

'See, what I'm thinking is – *BURP!* – why do I need to work for Ms Stranglebum when she could be the one who works for me? She was a pretty good evil villain –'

'Pretty good?' Pamela-Monkey shrieked again. 'I was the best evil villain. The BEST!'

'You're literally a monkey,' I pointed out.

'As I was saying,' Ernie continued, 'she was all right up until she turned into a monkey, but I could still use her talents. With my genius at the head of Minerva, and this ruby in my hands, I could rule the – *BURPPPP!* – world. Nobody could stop me!'

'That's where you're wrong! Because I've got myself a genius brain too, see?' Lenny said, pointing to his gargoyle-y head.

Ernie smirked and shook his head. 'Ah yes, Lennox Tuchus. What exactly do you think *you* can do to stop me?'

'I souped-up my brain, just like yours! We're super-brain twins. But I'm the good one and you're the evil one.'

'A super-brain? Lenny, you managed to get

yourself stuck in the body of a gargoyle.'

'Oh yeah, that. Bit of an accident. But my super-brain will sort things out, evil brain twin.'

'We are not – *BURP!* – brain – *BURP!* – twins,' Ernie burped.

'We are! I used that neuron-brainifying helmet right there,' Lenny said, pointing.

Ernie grinned. 'You mean *this* helmet?' He bent down and picked up a wire with a plug on the end. 'You mean this *unplugged* helmet?'

Pamela-Monkey started jumping up and down and chittering in her pod.

'Yeah, *that* helmet!' Lenny said. 'So I have a genius brain too! And any moment now it's going to come up with another genius plan to stop you!'

'Lenny,' I said, nudging him.

'Shh, not now. My genius brain is thinking . . .'

'But, Lenny –'

'*Shh!*'

Ernie rolled his eyes. 'Give him a moment – he'll get there.'

I nudged Lenny again. 'The Neuron Accelerator helmet™ wasn't –'

Lenny slapped his hands to his head, then gasped. 'Hang on a minute!'

Here we go.

'The neuron thingy . . . if it wasn't plugged in, how have I become so geniusly[sic] clever?'

Ernie studied his fingernails. 'You haven't. You're as stupid as you ever were.'

'Hey! He wasn't *that* stupid! You're the one who used to eat your own shoelaces, *Ernie*!'

Ernie glared, then farted, but it was Lenny who looked crestfallen.

'So . . . all those things I did . . . that wasn't my super-brain?'

'No,' Ernie said.

'Fool!' Pamela-Monkey shouted.

'Still a monkey, Pamela!' I snapped back.

Lenny didn't respond for a moment, then said, very quietly, 'I'm not clever, am I? I'm not clever at all.'

'He's finally got it!' Ernie said. 'I'm sorry, Lenny, but you are still completely stupid and absolutely worthless.'

'That's not true!' I shouted. 'You are clever, Lenny! You did all those things with your regular brain! You worked out how to get across town as a gargoyle, and blast in to save us in those rocket boots, and how to confuse the robot owls so their heads shot off –'

'Actually, the head thing was more of a happy accident,' Lenny interjected.

'And you calculated that you had to smash into me to get the Giant Ruby into the transmogrifier pod –'

'Well, now that I think about it, I don't remember doing all that much *calculating*. It was more of a hunch really.'

I gasped. 'I knew it! We'll discuss *that* later. But, anyway, what I'm saying is it was all you, Lenny. You came up with all those plans – well, most of them, but you know what I mean. Your regular brain has always been super in its own way. *You* have always been super. Because you have the biggest heart, Lennox Tuchus. You didn't think about your own safety coming here; you thought only of helping us!'

Lenny sniffled. 'I suppose that is true.'

'Oh, Lenny, you didn't need to change who you are; you just needed to change the way you look at yourself.' I sighed. 'Maybe I needed to do that too. But I see it now, Lenny. Look at Ernie – his brain might be oh-so-powerful, but what does that matter if he doesn't use it alongside his heart?'

Lenny didn't say anything for ages. Then he grinned at me. 'You called me super.'

'Yes, all right. Don't make a big deal about it.' I turned to Ernie. 'Ernie, I know Stranglebum changed your brain, but she didn't change your heart. I know our Ernie is inside you still. Our sweet, kind, shoelace-eating, glue-licking, funny Ernie. Ernie who could burp the alphabet – well, the bit of the alphabet he could remember anyway– and who would always check on kids if they were sad in class, and would pretend those big slabs of ham at lunch were his tongue and make everyone laugh. No Corruption Contraption™ could change all that. I miss that Ernie. I bet, if you're honest, you miss him too.'

'Nope, pretty happy as I am, actually.'

'I don't believe you. You can't be happy being this other Ernie. You could rule the world, but what's that worth if you have no friends?'

'Don't listen to her!' Pamela-Monkey shrieked. 'Think of the power!'

Ernie forced a great big smile on his face and said, 'Don't need friends. I have an evil monkey-lady and a giant moon-slicing ruby now. And yes, I'm happy. Very happy, thank you very much.'

'Ernie – our Ernie – would never have threatened to shrink his friends to the size of an amoeba, or robbed a museum, or tried to take over the world. Our Ernie wouldn't want to do any of that. He'd find it all too exhausting. Too lonely. So, I ask you again, are you happy doing this, Ernie? Honestly?'

He nodded.

'Honestly? You don't look very sure.'

'Of course he's happy!' Pamela-Monkey shouted. 'That other Ernie was an idiot!'

'I liked Other Ernie,' I said. 'He was caring and kind and funny, and I can't believe that he's happy being this mean, horrible version. Are you happy, Ernie?'

He nodded again. Then stopped and shook his head. Then fell to his knees, the Shrink-Your-Enemy-To-Amoeba-Size spray™ slipping from his hand. Then he started sobbing. Very loudly and very snottily.

'I don't think I want to be an evil super-brain villain any more. I just wanted people to stop thinking I was stupid. I'm always bottom in everything!'

'I understand,' Lenny-in-Gregor's-body said kindly.

'You're not stupid, either of you!' I said. 'Because you know what else I've realized? Scoring loads of points in tests can never tell you your real worth. Your true value comes from your actions – what you do and how you treat people. And both of you come right at the top for that.'

'We do?' Ernie sniffled.

'Well, ignoring the fact that you stole the Giant Ruby of Kathmandu and almost drowned

a load of grannies – yes, you do!'

Pamela-Monkey started jumping about and banging on the glass with her furry little fists.

'You have *got* to be kidding me! Let me out so we can take over the world!'

'Zip it, monkey!' I snapped. 'He said he didn't want to.'

'What I *do* want to do,' Ernie continued, 'is take a little nap . . . It's very tiring being so evil all the time.'

Pamela-Monkey shrieked with fury. 'No! Let me out of here, you idiot!'

Ernie looked at her with blotchy eyes.

'I am NOT an idiot!' he said. And then he farted and wailed some more, and started chewing his shoelace.

'Oh, Ernie,' I said, and leaned down to give him a hug.

Just as Gregor-in-Lenny's-body shot him with the stun gun.

CHAPTER 29

LENNY-IN-GREGOR'S-BODY

'**W**hat did you do that for?' gasped Agatha, looking from the frozen Ernie to Gregor-in-my-body and back to frozen Ernie again.

Gregor-in-my-body rolled his eyes. Well, my eyes.

'Because he's evil and wants to take over the world! *Obviously.*'

Agatha scowled. 'Did you not hear him when he said he doesn't want to be an evil villain any more? He literally just came back to our side!'

'Did he? Ah. I *might* have switched off by tha' point. You do have a wee tendency to go on a bit, lassie.'

'*Go on*? I was helping Ernie reach a moment of self-realization, so he didn't run off and become a **TERRIBLE EVIL CRIME BOSS**! Tell him, Lenny!'

'Tell him what, Agatha?'

'Lennox Tuchus, were you even listening to me?'

I gulped. 'Yes?'

'Then what did I say?'

'What did you say when?'

'Just now! To Ernie! My inspirational and moving speech.'

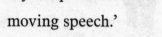

'Ooh yes! I know! Something about ham?'

Agatha glared at me. 'I was pointing out the importance of finding happiness in the truest version of yourself!'

'Really? I could have sworn you said something about ham. But, as we're talking about the truest versions of ourselves, do you think Gregor and I could change back?'

'Cannae do that just now, laddie,' Gregor said. 'Agatha's been bletherin' on fer so long, the **TERRIBLE EVIL CRIME BOSSES** have defrosted.'

Gregor was right. From the conference room came the sound of groaning as the villains started to come round from the effects of the stun gun.

'Oh, typical!' Agatha said, as if it wasn't her that had been wasting time.

Pamela-Monkey began jumping up and down and banging on the glass of her pod again.

'I'm in here, evil bosses! Release me at once!'

'She's starting to get right on my nerves,' Agatha said.

Monkey-Boss saw Pamela-Monkey, charged into the laboratory and pressed his face to the glass. 'Manuel . . . you can speak?!'

'It's me, Pamela! Manuel's in the other one!'

In the second pod, Manuel had taken off both of Pamela's shoes and was chewing her feet.

'Manuel, what have they done to you, my poor fur-baby?' Monkey-Boss cried, then he lunged at the button and the door opened.

'I'm not Manuel!' Pamela-Monkey said, leaping on to his shoulder, clutching the Giant Ruby in one paw. 'Attack the children!' she screeched. 'Get the girl first – I simply cannot *bear* to listen to any more of her speeches!'

Gregor-in-my-body shrugged at Agatha. 'Wha' did I tell ye?'

Monkey-Boss grabbed Agatha by her collar. Agatha struggled to get free, but he held on tight as the rest of the **TERRIBLE EVIL CRIME BOSSES** and Mr Whip charged into the laboratory.

My hero instincts kicked in once again. Well done, hero instincts! I sprang forward on my gargoyle-y legs and grabbed the Shrink-Your-Enemy-To-Amoeba-Size spray™ from the floor.

'Leave Agatha alone! She might go on and on, but that's just who she is! Now who wants to get amoebified?'

All the **TERRIBLE EVIL CRIME BOSSES** and Mr Whip gasped.

Agatha then interrupted my heroic moment by saying, 'Lennox Tuchus, I would just like to point out that I do *not* go on and on. If anything, it is your poor attention span that's the problem. If you were just able to focus, you'd probably realize that –'

'Agatha,' I interrupted back, 'do you want to talk about this now, or do you want me to shrink the **TERRIBLE EVIL CRIME BOSSES**?'

She swallowed. 'OK, amoebify their evil crime butts.'

'Amoebify their evil crime butts *what*?'

'Amoebify their evil crime butts, *please.*'

'That's better. Now which button do I push?'

Let's be honest, I'd never had much luck with buttons. My technique of hitting the first one I saw had met with mixed success. And there were just so many unnecessary buttons on this thing!

Pamela-Monkey jumped on top of Monkey-

Boss's head. 'Stop him! Stop the idiot gargoyle-boy!'

I decided to use my trusty spy-detective instincts, closed my eyes and chose a button at random.

'Why are you closing your eyes?!' Agatha said. '*Open them*!'

I did so and took aim.

'No one calls me an idiot gargoyle-boy,' I said in a very cool hero voice, and pushed the button.

I hit the Monkey-Boss right between the eyes. I was actually aiming for Pamela-Monkey, but it did the trick. There was a blinding flash and he completely disappeared with a little *poof*!

I'd done it! I had hit the right button! No one could ever doubt my random button-pushing ever again!

Pamela-Monkey fell to the ground, and the Giant Ruby rolled over to Gregor-in-my-body's feet. He snatched it up quickly and said, 'So beautiful!' Then gave it a lick.

'*Nooooooo!*' Pamela-Monkey shouted, angrily jumping up and down on her little paws, which was actually kind of cute. 'Give me back my Giant Ruby and my evil crime boss!'

'Don't squash me, Manuel!' came the tiny, squeaky voice of the amoebified Monkey-Boss.

'I'm not Manuel!' Pamela-Monkey shouted at the floor. Then she turned to the other bosses and said, 'What are you lot waiting for? Get them!'

'Watch out!' Gregor-in-my-body shouted as Mr Whip led the bosses towards me, but they could do nothing about the sharp-shooting skills of Lenny Tuchus. I took them out one after the other.

Flash. Flash. Flash.

Poof! Poof! Poof!

'Help!' came a chorus of squeaky voices.

Pamela-Monkey darted about the room as I tried to aim at her. 'Jump on!' she shouted to the now-amoeba-sized Mr Whip and the **TERRIBLE EVIL CRIME BOSSES.**

'It's over, Stranglebum,' Agatha said. 'Time to admit defeat.'

'Never! I have you right where I want you!'

'Seriously?' Agatha said. 'We have your Giant Ruby, your henchmen and henchwoman are now the size of single-celled organisms and you're stuck in the body of a monkey! I hope you've learned your lesson, Ms Stranglebum – never underestimate my friend Lenny Tuchus!'

'Don't you *ever* shut up?!' Pamela-Monkey shrieked. She must have realized that she'd been beaten, though, because she shook her furry monkey fist at us, shouted, 'This isn't over, you idiots! I'll be back!', and scampered out of the laboratory with all the teeny-tiny bosses squeaking on her back.

CHAPTER 30

AGATHA

So Lenny had saved the world. Again.

We stood for a moment, processing the events that had just occurred. We had got rid of Ms Stranglebum, all the **TERRIBLE EVIL CRIME BOSSES** *and* Mr Whip!

But we were left with quite a lot of tidying up to do. In particular, switching Lenny and Gregor back into the correct bodies and figuring out what we were going to do with the Giant Ruby of Kathmandu.

I opened the door to the pod and Manuel-in-Pamela's-body hopped out, jumped on to a desk and grabbed hold of the strip light. He then began swinging backwards and forwards, making happy *oo-oo-ah-ah* noises.

We were going to have to do something about that too, but first I turned to Gregor and Lenny. They'd been stuck long enough.

'Are you guys ready?'

Lenny-in-Gregor's-body jumped straight into the first pod. 'You betcha!'

'Gregor?'

Gregor-in-Lenny's-body was holding the ruby up to the light.

'It looks so . . . tasty,' he said, then bit down hard on it.

There was a crunch.

Then a yelp.

Gregor-in-Lenny's-body clutched his face and dropped the ruby. Manuel leaped down, swept it up, then climbed back up to the light and started swinging again.

'Oh, that's just brilliant!' I said. 'The monkey's got the Giant Ruby! What are we going to do now?'

'My tooth!' Lenny shouted. 'Gregor, did you

break my tooth?'

Gregor clamped
Lenny's hand over his
mouth and shook his head.

'That's it! I've had enough!'
Lenny cried. 'Get my butt in that
pod now, Gregor-in-my-body!'

'Aye,' said Gregor-in-
Lenny's-body, still
clutching his face. 'I
cannae take yer weak
jaws nae more!'

Lenny bent over and
pointed at his backside. 'And I can't
take any more of your bum-crevice moss!'

'Gah! Lenny! I did not need to see that!' I said.
'Gregor, please get in the pod.'

Gregor climbed into the transmogrification
pod and I slammed the door shut.

I hit the button and the air began to fizz and
crackle. There was a whoosh, and then a blinding

light, followed by some gurgling sounds from Gregor and Lenny.

'It feels like my brain is turning inside out!' Lenny yelped.

'Tell yer mammy I love her!' Gregor shouted out.

Then they both made this noise – '*UGUGUG GUGGG!*' – as their bodies began to judder violently and slightly bacony-scented smoke wafted out of the pods.

The juddering stopped.

Silence.

I pressed my palms on Lenny's pod and looked into his eyes, hoping to see my friend staring back. 'Has it worked?'

Lenny looked at his hands. Then at me.

'They're my handth! Pink and flethy and thoft! We've thwapped back! My bum ithn't itching. My kneeth are all thpringy! I feel thuper!'

He sprang out of the transmogrification pod. 'Wahooo! I'm back in my own body! I wath getting tho thick of being a gargoyle!'

'You were *what*?' I asked.

'I wath tho thick . . .' Lenny repeated, then trailed off. 'Argh! Ith my tooth! Gregor thmathed my tooth! And now I can't thpeak properly!'

'Aye, sorry aboot that.' Gregor stepped out of the other pod. 'I have to admit, it does feel pretty good to be back in ma own body,' he said, stretching and touching his toes.

'Did anybody hear a whistling sound?' I asked.

'Aye, I heard it too!' said Gregor, a puzzled look on his face.

'What *is* it?' I asked.

'It'th my tooth!' Lenny shouted. 'Which *you* thmathed! I can't thpeak without whithling!'

'Shush!' I said.

'I can't help it!' Lenny said. 'It'th my tooth gap!'

'Not that! I think I hear footsteps.'

We turned to the door just as it opened. Gregor

froze immediately because standing there was Dr Errno. His mouth dropped to his knees when he saw us.

'There you are! There's been a search party . . .'

He trailed off and his eyes began darting about. 'Wh-what is going on in here?' he stammered. 'Was the monkey that just ran up the stairs something to do with you?'

His eyes boggled about some more. 'Wh-wh-what . . . No, really, what is going on? What happened to all those robot librarian owls?!'

His eyes fell on still-stunned Ernie. 'Ernest Strewdel, stop chewing your shoelaces! We've been looking for you three ever since you went missing from the museum!'

His mouth dropped to his ankles when he saw Manuel-in-Pamela's-body swinging from the strip light. 'Ms Stranglebum?' he said. 'What are you doing?'

'She's been giving us extra tuition,' I said

quickly, beckoning her to come down. 'Isn't that right, Ms Stranglebum?'

Manuel-in-Pamela's-body dropped to the floor, scratched her bum, then sauntered over to a *very* surprised-looking Dr Errno.

'Extra tuition . . . b-b-but what is all this equipment? Is this Minerva stuff? Is that a *gargoyle*?'

Dr Errno looked deep into Manuel-in-Pamela's-body's eyes, searching for the answer. But he didn't reply because he was a monkey.

Instead, he started picking around in Dr Errno's ear hair, presumably looking for fleas and ticks to munch on.

'Oh, Ms Stranglebum!' gasped Dr Errno.

'Dr Errno,' I said. No answer. 'Dr Errno?'

He still didn't reply. He was sort of leaning into the ear-picking with his eyes closed.

'Dr Errno!' I said a little louder. 'I think you ought to see what Ms Stranglebum has in her other hand.'

His eyes snapped open. 'Pamela! That's the ruby that was stolen from the museum! The Giant Ruby of Kathmandu! You found it!'

Manuel-in-Pamela's-body started stroking Dr Errno's head and making soft grunting noises.

'I don't think Ms Stranglebum is quite herself, sir,' I said.

Dr Errno slowly shook his head. 'She seems perfectly . . . wonderful to me!'

'Do you think we should call the police?' I asked.

'Yes, at once! They must be informed that Ms Stranglebum has found the Giant Ruby! Oh bravo, Pamela, bravo!'

Manuel-in-Pamela's-body must have sensed Dr Errno was pleased with him, because he patted himself on the head. Dr Errno took his hand and steered him to the doorway.

'You three, stay here. I'll inform your parents that you've been found, and tell them to come and collect you.' As he walked out, he said, 'Poor Cleaner Wiener is going to have one heck of a job tidying up down here.'

Once he was gone, Lenny said, 'Ith Thtranglebum going to get the credit for finding the ruby?'

'Yes, Lenny, I think she is.'

'And no one ith going to know we thaved the world *again*?'

'No, Lenny, they're not. But we'll know. We'll know that we foiled Pamela Stranglebum's evil plan. And that we managed to stop a flock of killer robot librarians from lasering us to death. And that we took out a load of **TERRIBLE EVIL CRIME BOSSES** *and* a terrible PE teacher. And saved

Ernie from a life of villainy. As well as all the other kids who would have been recruited if Minerva's plan had gone ahead. We'll know that we did that. Just us. Just as we are. You, me and Gregor. You don't get into the spy-detective business for the glory –'

Lenny let out a frankly massive yawn.

'LENNOX TUCHUS!'

Lenny jumped. 'Huh, what?'

'Are you listening to me?'

'Thorry, Agatha. I kind of thwitched off a bit there.'

'Ye *do* go on a bit, lassie,' Gregor said.

'But we wouldn't change you,' Lenny added quickly.

I smiled. 'I wouldn't change you either.'

He gave me a massive grin.

'Apart from that whistling noise your mouth keeps making. That's going to get quite annoying.'

'Thorry, Agatha, are you thtill thpeaking?'

'I don't know, Lenny. Are you still whistling?'

CHAPTER 31

LENNY-BACK-TO-PLAIN-OLD-LENNY

Lots of things happened after the battle in the laboratory.

Firstly, I got my tooth fixed.

Secondly, let's just say some spy-detectives and a gargoyle might have smashed up all the Minerva equipment so none of it worked any more (except the Truth Trunks™ – Agatha kept those: she said they'd be very useful in our line of work). Because Ms Stranglebum had scampered off in the body of Manuel the crime monkey, with Mr Whip and the **TERRIBLE EVIL CRIME BOSSES** living as amoebas in her fur, there was no one around to fix any of it.

Dr Errno didn't seem to mind, though. He was too busy being smoochy with Manuel-in-Pamela's-body.

As the school was still keen to help the environment, a new task force was established, the Green Team, which was fronted by Ernie Strewdel. He offered his super-brain to help save the ice caps, the rainforests and the blue-footed booby, one recycled toilet roll at a time.

After every mission, Agatha always has to have a debriefing session to talk about what we've learned so we can be better spy-detectives moving forward. It's all a bit boring in my opinion, but I guess that's because I pretty much know all there is to know about spy-detectivizing. I've saved the world twice now and Agatha hasn't even saved it once, so I guess she still has a lot to learn. And, because I am not only a hero but an excellent and generous leader, I guess I don't mind going back over the main points of my super-heroic world-saving if it helps her out.

This time, our meeting took place the weekend after we'd defeated Ms Stranglebum, and Agatha, Gregor and I were in my bedroom.

Gregor had been very keen we met at my house. While Agatha and I were sitting cross-legged in the den we had built using a bedsheet and some pegs, Gregor was at the window, sighing and watching my mum hang out the rest of the washing.

'Mistakes,' Agatha said, shaking her head. 'Far too many mistakes.'

'Don't be too hard on yourself,' I said kindly. 'It worked out all right in the end.'

'That may be true, but moving forward I would like you to reflect on some of the actions that you took –'

'You mean my super-heroic actions? I've reflected and I am very pleased with them all.'

'I'm talking about the time you went spy-detectoring without me and transmogrified yourself into a gargoyle.'

'Yes, and I don't want you to feel bad about

that. I know you were very focused on getting to the top of the leader board. I do not blame you for deserting me. I'm not saying it was *exactly* as if you pushed the button yourself –'

'That's because *you* pushed the button!'

'But *was* it me, Agatha? Or was it really the cruel hand of abandonment that reached out?'

'It was YOU!' she spluttered.

'Only because you weren't there to stop me. You were so busy worrying about proving you were the best, you forgot how to be my best friend. And, when you're not around to be my best friend, bad things happen.'

Agatha opened her mouth and I thought she was going to come out with some more nonsense about it being my fault, but instead she closed it again and did the tiniest of nods.

'I suppose that's true. I'm sorry, Lenny. You're right. It's just that those pedal points made me feel like I was worth something. I thought being the best would make my parents proud of me. But I should never have forgotten about you.'

'You don't have anything to prove, Agatha. Deep down you know your parents are proud of you. I reckon it's more that you needed to be proud of yourself.'

She raised an eyebrow. 'You reckon, do you?'

'Yup! It's like you told me and Ernie – you don't always have to be the best at everything. You can just be you. That's enough.'

Agatha smiled. 'Thank you, Lenny.'

'And you are my occasionally trustworthy assistant.'

'Your WHAT?!'

I grinned. 'And the bestest person I know. Seriously, Agatha, you should be proud of yourself. I'm proud of you.'

'Hmmm,' she hmmed. 'With that in mind, there is something we should have done a lot sooner. Follow me.'

We scrambled out of the den, leaving Gregor at the window, and Agatha led me downstairs and out into the street.

'What are we doing?'

'We have another mission, Lennox Tuchus. A very important one.'

'Another?!' Frankly, I was still getting over the last one. Then a thought struck me. 'Ooohhh! Is it the aliens?'

'It's never the aliens, Lenny. But I wanted to do something to make up for the fact that I didn't listen to you at the beginning of our last mission. To show you I'm sorry that I wasn't a very good friend.'

Agatha checked her watch. 'He should be here any minute.'

'Who?' I asked, but she didn't need to answer because from round the corner I spotted a car I recognized.

'It's my dad!' My heart swelled in my chest so much I thought I might burst.

'I gave him a call. We thought maybe you might like us to teach you to ride a bike.'

THE END

Sam Copeland is an author, which has come as something of a surprise to him. He is from Manchester and now lives in London with two smelly cats, three smelly children and one relatively clean-smelling wife. He is the author of the bestselling *Charlie Changes Into a Chicken*, which spawned two sequels: *Charlie Turns Into a T-Rex* and *Charlie Morphs Into a Mammoth*. His other books include *Uma and the Answer to Absolutely Everything* and *Greta and the Ghost Hunters*. With Jenny Pearson, he has also written *Tuchus & Topps Investigate: The Underpants of Chaos*. Despite legal threats, he refuses to stop writing.

Follow Sam online:
www.sam-copeland.com
@stubbleagent

Jenny Pearson has been awarded six mugs, one fridge magnet, one wall plaque and numerous cards for her role as Best Teacher in the World. When she is not busy being inspirational in the classroom, she would like nothing more than to relax with her two young boys, but she can't as they view her as a human climbing frame. Her first novel, *The Super Miraculous Journey of Freddie Yates*, was shortlisted for the Waterstones Children's Book Prize and the Costa Children's Book Award, and won the Laugh Out Loud book award. Her other titles are *The Incredible Record Smashers* and *Grandpa Frank's Great Big Bucket List* and *Operation Nativity*. With Sam Copeland, she has also written *Tuchus & Topps Investigate: The Underpants of Chaos*.

Follow Jenny online:
www.jennypearsonauthor.com
@J_C_Pearson

Katie Kear is a British illustrator based in the Cotswolds and has been creating artwork for as long as she can remember. She loves creating new worlds and characters, and hopes to spread joy and happiness with her illustrations!

As a child, her favourite memories always involved books. Whether it was reading her first picture books with her mother before bed and imagining new stories for the characters, or as an older child reading chapter books into the night, she remembers always having a love for them! This is what made her pursue her career in illustration.

Katie is a graduate of the University of Gloucestershire, with a first-class BA Honours degree in illustration. In her spare time she loves drawing, adventures in nature, chocolate, stationery, the smell of cherries and finding new inspirational artists!

Robin Boyden is an illustrator who also lives in the Cotswolds and thinks Katie is copying him. He lives with his partner and their sensitive cockapoo, Lupin, who is his muse. Robin has always been drawing – ALWAYS. He began his professional career aged six, when he created his own comic and attempted to auction it off in class. With characters such as 'Tony the tennis racket' and 'Henry the sad orange', it was a shock that the comic went unsold. He is clearly not appreciated in his own time.

He also has a first-class degree (stop copying Katie, seriously) from University College Falmouth, and a master's apparently.

When not drawing, Robin likes to grow plants and pretend to know what bird is sitting in that tree over there. Robin thinks *The Wind In The Willows* is great and wishes he could write a book about Christmas.